WITCH AND PEACE

BETTINA M. JOHNSON

Aqua Raven Publishing

CHAPTER 1

I slowly turned over on the beach towel, stretching my arms above my head then tucking them behind my neck, luxuriating in the warm breeze as it gently caressed my body—the smell of the surf tickling my senses.

Rolling over onto my side, I traced one hand over the surface of the sand, each grain a gentle abrasive marvel on my fingertips as my eyes tracked Lorcan's approach. He rose out of the surf, his body glistening, as the sun's rays made the droplets on his torso sparkle. He slowly made his way toward me with a seductive stride making my heart rate hitch in anticipation.

Dropping to his knees in front of me, he leaned forward as beads of water cascaded down his chest. His gaze bore into mine, warm and gentle yet hinting of wild things to come, as he smiled and brought his lips mere inches from my own. His sweet breath was a heady mixture of bacon and coffee, and I knew his kiss would render me...

Bacon?

Coffee?

My brain slammed on the brakes, pulling me slowly out of my reverie, rendering me fully awake. I was ensconced in my bed, sans beach towel, but wrapped in my blanket. There was nary a grain of sand in sight unless I counted the grimy bits set in the corners of my eyes. I began rubbing to chase away the last of what would undoubtedly have been one heck of a sweet dream. Taking stock of my situation, I concluded that the smells emanating from downstairs were most assuredly that of bacon and coffee, and I may even detect eggs to boot.

I sat up and peered around the room, looking for my cat, Wicked. She was nowhere around, but my open door gave me a hint of her whereabouts.

Glancing at the window, I noted it was still fairly dark outside, so I tracked my eyes over to my alarm clock. Six a.m.? Really?

It took me less than ten minutes to make a bathroom pit stop, don some slippers, and wander downstairs, where I heard the distinctive sound of human conversation. Considering I lived alone with my mother, Adelaide, as my roommate—and this a recent occurrence, I began to ponder just to whom she was conversing. That I had two ghosts popping in and out of my life made me consider it might be they with whom mom was having her lively discourse.

Shuffling along, I made my way to the kitchen and came to an abrupt halt.

Adelaide was, indeed, chatting away, but it was Lorcan she was speaking to—he, the man in my dreams, until I remember he'd proposed and was, in fact, my fiancé. I still am not processing this. Wicked was sitting on the counter watching Lorcan flip eggs while Adelaide was draining the bacon, carefully straining the liquid fat into a lard jar while trapping the bits in a strainer as any proper southern lady would. What had me agog—or who, rather—was sitting at my kitchen table, in my spot, eating a heaping plate of pancakes, drinking the aforementioned coffee—and using my mug!

"Nempf!" I think that was the sound that came out of me, anyway.

"Lily! Darling. Good morning," Adelaide said, smiling at me as she placed the tray of bacon back in the oven. We must be feeding an army because another plate of bacon was ready for consumption on the counter.

"Hey, baby." This from Lorcan, who expertly cracked another two eggs in the heavily-buttered pan.

I remained rooted to the floor.

"What's wrong, love?" Adelaide noticed my mien and became mildly concerned since I still had my mouth hanging open and couldn't form any coherent words.

I thrust my arm out—elbow locked, palm facing up with fingers tight, the thumb cocked and pointing in the direction of my chair.

"Nmeh."

"That's Abner, dear." She replied.

My brows went down into a deep V, and I manage to speak appropriately.

"I know that's Abner. But what is he doing here, and why is he in my spot?"

Abner paused from shoveling pancakes in his pie hole faster than a train conductor stoking the burner on a coal train. He responded with yet another utterance that would make Captain Obvious proud. "I'm eatin' break-fast."

Yes. Abner actually said break then fast.

"Why are you eating it here, again?"

"Gotta get them seedlings in the ground now that we

are full on the spring planting season. Time is money." Abner replied.

Seedlings? Spring?

I looked out the window to see if anything had changed since I last made a note of the weather conditions. Yesterday evening, before I crept upstairs to bed, my life seemed as ordinary as my life could be with the assurances that we were in the middle of a late March ice storm. I was secure in the knowledge that not much had altered. The entire landscape looked like Jack Frost did a jig with Queen Elsa making the landscape safe for the residents of Arendelle. In other words:

"There are icicles everywhere, and the ground looks like permafrost."

In that instant, another strong gust rattled my windows as ice plinked against the panes. Even the fireplace sizzled as errant moisture reached the flames, emphasizing my point.

That's the thing with the weather in the north Georgia mountains—things could change from year to year. One March, you could have cookouts and plant flowers while you put away your winter clothing, while the following year would find yourself huddled around your fireplace dreaming of global warming. This year was one for the record books as far as snow and cold were concerned.

"That's why I'm in here. No sense in planting when the ground's still a frozen like."

I slowly blinked as my face went blank. It took me a few minutes to process the fact that Abner had just told me he was here to plant. You know what? Yeah. I needed to stop thinking because I could feel my brain cells melting, never to regenerate again.

"Abner has seedlings ready for your greenhouse, Lily,"

Adelaide explained. "Then when this cold weather finally snaps, he can move them to your planting bed."

"Whatever happened to my peas? Are they dead?" I asked, remembering the little green nubs we added to the soil back in February when Donald Murphy, my friend and an avid gardener, insisted they needed to be interred to the ground lest we miss their planting schedule.

Hold up. Was my greenhouse usable?

"No. Peas know when to come up. They will jest wait for a spell until the soil tells them it's time. Then there's no holding them back. Don't you worry none." Abner nodded to himself.

I wasn't worried in the slightest. I didn't even know I had a functioning greenhouse, having not had the time to explore the little building, barely giving it a cursory glance or two since moving in a few months back.

"But, Abner, as much as I get a little thrill rush through me, every time I see your face—or hear your voice—what are you doing here? In my kitchen? Don't you have a home somewhere nearby or something you need to worry about?" Or heaven forbid! A wife? And that thrill coursing in my veins had more to do with thoughts of murder than any other emotion I might be experiencing.

Abner, however, ignorant of this, looked pleased and a bit touched by my concern. I wasn't about to correct his assumptions.

"Lily, Abner lives here on the property. I told you he is our handyman. I has been for years! He lives in that tiny cabin behind the greenhouse."

There is a tiny cabin behind the greenhouse?

"Can't see it for the kudzu growing over it. But I like it the same. Exceptin' when the weather gets this cold. With all my handymanin' and gardenin' I plumb forgot to chop any firewood last Autumn. Now, well the place gets cold, and my heater is on its last legs."

I looked over to Lorcan who seemed as shocked at this news as I was.

"Abner! You should have told me. I would have brought you some. We can take care of it today." I loved Lorcan for his big heart, and the rest of the town wasn't too far behind me.

I sighed inwardly and continued, "Let me know what kind of heater you need, Abner, and I will get one and have it installed. In the meantime, I guess you can stay here."

I did not just say that.

"Oh! No, no. Got some windows to fix over at Lorcan's shop and I'm gonna spend the day there. Then this evening I have my poker group. Not even an ice storm can stop us from meeting! Gordy said I could spend the night, so I'm good."

You might be, Abner, but did anyone inform Sheila? I had a feeling Gordy was about to be in the doghouse. Or not. I mean, Abner does have some sort of appeal. If you like Captain Obvious one-liners that grate on your last nerve.

"Plus, Stu is stayin' over and he's the one givin' me the ride to Gordy and Sheila's. She put on a big pot of beef stew for us and is stayin' out of our way. I heard she's with Shirley tonight and they're playing the Bunco. Shirley has some kind of troubles, and Sheila is tryin' to distract her."

I think it's just Bunco, but what did I know?

Stu is a part time mechanic that works for Lorcan. He's Sheila and Shirley's little brother. A sweet guy if a bit slow, but he's another man in this town with a good heart. You just had to wait two weeks for him to come up with the right words to finish one sentence.

He's also our mayor.

Shocking. I know.

Small Georgia towns. Gotta love them.

"Is Shirley well? Is there anything we can do?" I asked, hoping it wasn't a serious matter as I already felt stretched thin with my own troubles.

"Don't rightly know. Gordy and Sheila didn't say."

Sheila worked at Joe's Diner, my favorite food place in all Sweet Briar. Shirley, her big sister, was the town's EMT.

"Ok, then. Can I ask why then we have this little impromptu breakfast going on during an ice storm? Minus Abner being here?"

"Because I'm hungry, and you have a stocked fridge."

Ack!

I spun around to see the diminutive form of my great-grandmother, Adriana Dolce, standing behind me looking smug in her grey wool shawl covering her pajamas with fuzzy green slippers on her feet. Pajamas?

"Were you here all night? When did you get here? I'm confused." I said as I walked over to my chair and motioned Abner to get out of it. He did, grabbing his plate and almost absconding with my mug, but I was too quick for him.

I went to the sink, rinsed it, then poured myself a cup —black, like my mood—and stomped into the den where I curled up in my favorite chair.

Adelaide frowned at me as she handed a grateful Abner another mug of coffee. He nodded and grinned in appreciation.

Adriana continued. "I spent the night, and you'd know this if you hadn't have gone to bed at seven like a toddler."

"For your information, there is a winter storm going on, and I was up the previous night making sure we had candles and supplies while the lights kept flickering. I was waiting for a tree to come crashing through my roof with all that wind we had, and I am sleep-deprived. That still doesn't explain how you got here and when!"

"I've been here since Thursday." Adriana sniffed.

It was Saturday.

"I don't even." I took a sip of my coffee, grimaced, and stomped back into the kitchen, where I doctored my brew with heaps of sugar and cream.

"If you must know, my car broke down on Wednesday, and I had it towed to your lover boy's place. I spent the night at June's then came here by foot. You locked your door so that I couldn't get in, but Wicked saw me looking in your back door and opened it for me."

I glared at my cat, who seemed amused by the interplay. Don't ask how Wicked managed to open a locked door. I have given up trying to figure it out.

"I called Keisha and informed her I'd not be home until the storm let up and just caught her before she left for the day. She locked the house up, making sure she'd turned my heat up, so my pipes don't freeze. Then she made it safely back to her place because I checked in on her. So, with no pressing matters to attend to at home, I decided I'd stay here."

Wait. No pressing... "How can you say that? What about Grandfather Antonio? You can't just leave him alone with no one to care for him! How can you be so cruel?!" I was shocked that my great-grandmother would be so inconsiderate and downright negligible. Keisha, too, since she was his nurse and all.

"Oh, he'll be fine. Or not. Either he will be warm and toasty, or the heat will fail, and he will freeze to death." Adriana said this with a gleam of amusement in her eyes, causing me to grasp I was being trifled with. She was joking, obviously. I think.

8

I kept staring at her until she finally rolled her eyes so hard, teenagers around the world would be envious.

"Ok, fine. You big baby. He's at his cabin in the woods near Pot Gap Ridge near Dick's Knob."

Did you understand any of that? I was afraid even to ask.

"Why is he alone in a cabin in the woods, on the top of a mountain, during an ice storm?" I asked, fearing the answer would be something beyond my scope of comprehension.

Adriana waltzed into the kitchen, grabbed a handful of bacon, and began to consume it loudly.

"Who said he was alone? Mortimer is with him."

Mortimer was a vampire. This should make any sane person quake, but I am no sane person. Especially since finding out I was a witch and came from a crackpot family of witches. All of them crazy, and most of them within thirty square miles of the town of Sweet Briar, Georgia, where I now lived.

Long story short, I was born here. Left with my aunt, who I thought was my mother at the time, lived for years in the upstate of New York, in the Catskill Mountains, then upon her death, returned "home" to Sweet Briar per her instructions. Only to find out I come from a dynasty of witches, some of whom are dark—and in Adriana's case, pure evil. Ok, so I am a dark witch as well. Please don't hold it against me. It does not mean we are malevolent or do horrible acts with bubbling cauldrons at the ready. It means we battle dark forces with our unique ability to control dark magic.

Despite my ignorance in all things witch, growing up, I've quickly caught up, and think I am getting rather proficient at spellcasting if I may say so!

Mortimer is a friendly vampire whose parents have

retired and live in a retirement condo village in Florida. I know, I know. Who knew vampires would ever retire and move to the Sunshine State, all things considered? Apparently, the older a vampire got, the less affected by the sun they became. I guess it didn't hurt that he was part shifter as well.

Believe me, I am still trying to get a handle on the paranormal world myself having grown up, assumably a human.

"Why is Mortimer with Antonio? And now? With the weather this bad?"

Sighing in exasperation, Adriana picked up her coffee and downed it in one gulp, then slammed the mug on the counter.

"Because they are tracking the new warden of the prison so they can find out the secret entrance, sneak in, then transport me there. This way I can finally get answers out of Donna Fredricks before I choke the life out of her. Or die trying."

And that's how my weekend started, folks! Little did I know how much worse it was about to get.

CHAPTER 2

After a filling breakfast and another three cups of coffee, I decided I needed to shower and dress properly before we settled down to the impromptu meeting Adriana desired. Once I found out what she was up to, I wanted in. I, for one, was eager to move on Donna Fredricks and would gladly help my great-grandmother choke the life out of her. Ok, maybe just shove her around a tad before we tossed her into an inescapable and heavily-warded prison cell.

But still.

Lorcan settled onto the sofa to look on his iPad for heating units with Abner. Adriana and Adelaide, um, Mom, were cleaning up breakfast and would meet me back down in the den when I was finished with my ablutions. I really needed a shower. I had been keeping late nights, not just because of the high winds and pelting ice as the excuse I'd given Adriana, but due to my witchy lessons. Adelaide and I had been working to catch me up to the levels I should be at for my age. Every single day, seven days a week, without fail, we'd been at it.

One of the spells that had intrigued me to the point of distraction was a *come hither* spell where, when performed correctly, could have me whisking some unsuspecting victim to my side. I could call them with a mere summons, or alternatively, I could manifest in front of them when they least expected. All I needed was something of theirs to make the magic work. You can see why my being a Shadow Dancer, a tracker, able to pull magical essence from any witch who left a trail behind could be such a powerful talent!

I spent the last four days torturing my cat, making her appear in front of me when I used a bit of her fur, created the potion, and diligently practiced using it. Once second she was happily curled up in front of the fire, the next instant she was across the room at my feet. The look of surprise on her face was priceless. I waited until she'd settled herself in a new spot and dozed off before trying again. She was less amused the second time around and hissed at me. After an hour of the ongoing torment, she managed to find the vial of potion I'd concocted, her fur floating inside, and ran off with it. Hey! After some of the hijinks she's pulled on me, I decided she deserved a bit of teasing. I smiled now at the memory and looked down to find her at my feet—this time willingly.

I'd reached the foyer, Wicked on my heels as I climbed the stairs leading up. That's when I noticed she seemed tense, and her fur began to rise.

"What's with you?"

I tried not to be too alarmed when I heard a distinctly ominous grumble come out of her tiny furry body. Every single hair on her sleek black coat was now at full attention and she looked like a lint ball left in the dryer. It went into overdrive when I saw her ears flatten and her tail lash back and forth like a whip. What on earth? Reaching the top of the landing, I cautiously approached my bedroom door. Now I was on high alert because my witchy senses kicked in and I felt a presence. I knew with certainty I'd find someone—or something—on the other side of my door.

My magic switched on and I embraced it as it began to coil slowly up my core. My fingertips tingled and I waited until the sparks began dancing around them before going forward.

"You can stop your grandstanding, witch. You'd be a pile of dust before you lifted one of those pretty fingers in my direction."

The voice coming from my room was low and sultry—and familiar—but I couldn't place to whom it belonged. What now?

Trusting my cat and her precognition, I kept my hands free. Lifting my leg high, I kicked open the door.

Laying on my bed was the hottest woman I'd ever laid eyes on. And I didn't even play on that team! But this woman made Angelina Jolie, Jessica Alba, Charlize Theron, Rhianna, Keira Knightley, all the eighties' supermodels combined and that girl on the cover of Time Magazine with the beautiful face and haunting eyes look like a coven of ugly hags who people had no right gazing at lest they be turned to stone. Where did she come from? More importantly, why was she here—and in my bed?

"Don't look so shocked! After all, you were the one who left me here."

"I did? Sorry, but I think I'd remember leaving you lying in my bed. I might be sleep-deprived, but not *that* sleep-deprived!"

The pulchritudinous creature began to chuckle as she sat up, stretching her arms above her head. I barely kept my mouth from dropping open when I realized she wasn't wearing much if anything in the way of clothing. What is it with me and naked women? First Tarni, my distant siren cousin, now this one!

Realizing my mild discomfort at her condition, the lively being laughed outright and patted the mattress, motioning that I should join her. Uh, yeah, no thanks lady!

"Come on. You don't know what you're missing, love." She winked playfully at me and I blushed. Then I frowned. This was turning out to be a bizarre day and it wasn't even nine o'clock yet!

"Seriously, I've had a weird morning as it is, I really don't feel like playing games."

"Oh! Pooh. You're no fun at all. Games is what it's all about, sugar! Everything in life is one big game. Care to play with me now?"

My frown deepened and I placed my hands on my hips. I was going for severe, but the woman threw her head back and roared with more laughter.

"Who are you? And why are you in my room? And how did you get in here?" I demanded. Peering around, I searched for an access I might have left open, but the windows were shut tight. The front door was closed and locked when I just passed it a minute ago, so that was out.

"Silly, Lily. Perhaps you'd know me if I rhymed all the time? Wouldn't that be sublime? Or is it the unknown you fear which is why you dare not come near?"

Rhyme? What the heck was this crackpot going on about? The last time anyone around here had rhymed it had been... "Oh, my gosh! You're the book!"

"The one and only!" Jumping up off the bed, the gorgeous creature rushed over to me, throwing her arms around my body and gave me a massive hug. Then she grabbed my hands and lead me back over to the bed where she flopped down, dragging me with her, like we were about to have a slumber party.

"I've been waiting for just the right time to come out and speak with you. By the way, wrapping me up and shoving me in your closet wasn't a nice thing to do. Your closet needs organizing, and you have very little in the way of sexy lingerie, dear. A ratty grey sleep tee? Really? How in Heavens name do you plan on keeping that man of yours enthralled? You need a girl's fun day out, a shopping trip, and I want to take you on it." She squealed and began to titter in a bubbly kind of way.

I just blinked and tried my best to sit up, but Bubbles here, was not having it.

"Oh, no you don't. I've lots to discuss with you, but first things first. You need to shower and then I'm going to find just the right outfit for you to wear." Before I knew what had happened, I found myself flat on my back and pinned down by the beautiful amazon. I immediately began to fight her, and we tussled back and forth, which had me losing my pajama top in the battle. This went on for a bit until she flipped me once again, this time straddling me then leaned down so we were nose-to-nose—not to mention breast-to-breast—then she gave me an impudent victory grin.

"Now, how about that shower?"

I was about to push the woman off me with magic, however that's when Lorcan walked into my room. The look of incredulity on his face rendered me speechless, but not Bubbles. She gave Lorcan a sexy wink, turned back to me and kissed the tip of my nose. Then she cried, "Tag! You're it!"

"I DON'T KNOW what's going on. I told you already. She just showed up—or was in my room already, rather. I am so confused."

Didn't I say those very words earlier? Why did no one believe me?

"Baby, you were half naked in bed with another woman. Practically making out with her, and you are telling me you have no idea how she got into your room or when?"

"Lorcan Reid! Do not even try to make this something! I went upstairs, Wicked followed. I noticed the cat get all hinky and spooked so I went on high alert. Next thing I know I find a woman in my room and she has a penchant for nudity and games!"

"Don't you mean kinky, Squirt?" Adriana cackled evilly, and I threw her a look that could melt glaciers.

"Adriana! Leave her be. She's traumatized," Adelaide chided.

I would have replied with a scathing remark, but the woman of the hour chose that moment to come back into the dining room where we were all gathered—minus Abner, and I was grateful for that at least. Thankfully she was clothed, but the way she was sucking on the pudding pop and leering at Lorcan made my blood boil.

"Stop that! He's spoken for!"

Baring her teeth at me with a wicked grin, the demon slithered around the table, but not before running her hand through Lorcan's hair. He became momentarily dazed, and it was my turn to show some teeth. This just caused Bubbles—I still internalized that name since I had no other yet—to snort. Nosily sucking on her pop, she pulled out a chair and took a seat opposite me. Grabbing an apple off the table, she sniffed it then took a big bite. Talking around the mouthful of apple, she leaned back and introduced herself formally.

"The name's Pandora. But you can call me Dorie for short."

"Pandora? What, like the Greek mythology chick?" I asked.

"Yeah, only she's isn't the myth. What we have here is a crossroads demon." Adriana declared.

Dorie jumped up and made a curtsey before plunking back down and continuing to eat, alternating between the apple and licking her frozen treat in a disturbingly seductive way. Oh, so, I was right by thinking that about her just now, a demon. Lovely.

I smacked the back of Lorcan's head to help him clear it and leaned forward.

"Why did you hide out in my room this long, and why did you take the shape of a book to do...do...whatever the heck it is you do?"

"What I do is cause mischief and mayhem wherever I go. My favorite pastime is playing devil's advocate. I measure thirty-eight, twenty-three, thirty-six and stand at five foot nine and a quarter inch in my stocking feet. I also take souls, trading them for favors. I like walks in the park, trips to the mountains, nude beaches, and can ride a bull a full eight minutes without falling off. A real one—not a mechanical one. Oh! A few years ago, I had a wild love affair with a powerful vampire, but you've met him already. Thanks for setting him free by the way!"

She must mean Valgaard, an ancient vampire I had recently freed from being frozen in place, staked through the heart by wood. He was Caliente's father—Mortimer's lady friend. I still had to wrap my head around the fact that vampires not only existed, but apparently like to get it on.

"But why did you take the form of that book? What role do you play in this farce that is happening in our world, to my family, specifically? I mean, you were coveted by an ancient witch-part-shifter ancestor of ours who sold her soul to become a changeling, a vampire, and—"

I sat back so hard I almost knocked my chair backward in the process.

"You were the one she sold her soul to, weren't you? That's why she was trying to find and possess you!"

"Got it in one, sugar. Now. What do ya'll do around here for kicks? Or *who*?" She purred this while retuning her gaze to Lorcan, fluttering her eyelashes in the process.

"It's nice to meet you again after all these years, Pandora." Adelaide said quietly. "I did enjoy all the lessons you taught me but wished I had complete knowledge of the price to pay for playing with you."

"Oh, sugar. Your soul is intact. Never once did you ask to trade it for something I could give you. You were my favorite pupil, Adelaide. Charlie too. And Jess to some extent. You were such delightful inquisitive children! Thanks for not giving me to Lucretia when you had the opportunity. I think she'd have locked me away in a piece of jewelry by now and would be ruling this world like a tyrant tapping my power to do so."

That's right! My parents and Aunt Jessica taught the book, er, Pandora how to rhyme and played with her when she was in book form. I felt dizzy with all the dots I was connecting.

"So, what now?" I asked.

That's when a loud alarm sounded and Edith Plank, my resident ghost, popped in.

"We have trouble! Mortimer found the prison. He tracked the new warden from the prison board to an abandoned Phillips 66 on Old Lula Road. The guy opened a manhole around the back and took down the barrier spell, but then he clutched his chest and keeled over dead of an apparent heart attack. Mortimer and Antonio rushed over, but before he could reseal the cover, Antonio leaned forward and fell right in. Plop! Mortimer sent me to get all of you. He can't find Antonio anywhere. He's missing!"

And all this in the biggest ice storm to hit the south in forty years. Cue the menacing music. Things had already gone south, and it was going to turn out badly. I just knew it.

CHAPTER 3

"Can't this thing go any faster?" Adriana complained as she worried her hands in her lap.

I knew she was frantic to get to the site where Antonio apparently fell into a hole, probably landing him into the depths of the prison. I was desperate myself but didn't want to wind up sliding on the slick highway and barreling over a cliff. We were heading north toward North Carolina and climbing. My Jeep could handle just about anything I threw at it, but ice was ice.

"Everything is going to be fine. Mortimer is searching for him. I'm going as fast as I dare."

Lorcan had graciously given up the front seat to my great-grandmother and was stuffed in the back with Adelaide and Dorie, who was taking advantage of the situation by occasionally leaning into him and batting her eyelashes in a disturbing way. I'd taken to snapping my fingers at her whenever she crossed the line. Lorcan just looked miserable, like he'd rather have stayed behind—or run home to his parents.

Every time I caught his eye in the rearview mirror, I

blushed. I can't believe the first time my fiancé saw me almost completely naked, I happened to be in bed rough-housing with another woman—another semi-naked woman. This was going to cause all manner of issues down the road, I just knew it. What was wrong with Dorie anyway? And what the heck is a crossroads demon? We didn't have time for explanations after Edith's frenzied arrival, but I knew I'd have to address not only what Dorie is, but how she acts sooner rather than later. Not to mention, what did she want with me? Or was she back because Adelaide was as well?

It couldn't be just a need to give me fashion advice and go shopping. Right?

Like I needed another weird character to show up in my world and cause...whatever it is she planned on causing. Vampires. Shifters. Now a crossroad demon? Ugh!

"Slow down, Lily. I think you need to make the next turn if this GPS thingy on your phone is right." Adelaide told me. My poor mother was fused into my cat, Wicked, for twenty odd years. She needed to catch up a bit and she is still amazed we use phones for everything for communication to maps to photos. That one knocked her socks off.

"Lorcan, can you please try to focus and check the GPS?" Jumping in embarrassment—he'd been doing his best not to watch Dorie adjusting the buttons on her flimsy shirt—Lorcan fastened his eyes onto the GPS on my dashboard.

"Your mom is right, but I think it's the one just after this turn. The GPS on your Jeep seems to need an update or calibration or something because it looks different on the phone. "What town is this anyway? Tate City?"

"Yeah. If you can call it a town. It's more like a group of houses and a shack. Charming in a way, but hardly a town. Once we pass through the main area, we continue up Tate City Road until we run parallel to the Tallulah River. The old Phillips 66 is up a bit. Abandoned and easy to spot—or so said Mortimer. Holy cow but its icy out there! Why does Grandpa Antonio have a cabin way up here?"

"Hunting."

Adriana was terse, and drawn. I didn't blame her or get offended. She must be going insane with worry.

"I didn't know he was a hunter."

"Not animals. Mushrooms. Although he almost shot a wild turkey once. It tried to mate with his beagle mix, Daisy."

Ok, then.

"I didn't know you owned a beagle."

"We don't. She's been dead for decades. Although we still have her in one of the downstairs offices or guest rooms. Antonio had her stuffed, so she'd always be around. Odd one, your great-grandpa.

I didn't know what to say to that little revelation, so I kept my mouth shut for once.

"There!" Lorcan pointed, not that I needed him to. Not only was the old gas station the only thing on this lonely road, but Mortimer was also standing in the street, and you couldn't miss an almost seven-foot-tall vampire waving his arms to flag you down if you tried.

I parked and we exited the Jeep and immediately hunched over from the cold wind slapping into us. Why knew it could get this cold in March in Georgia? My goosebumps had goosebumps.

Mortimer didn't seem phased and was dress all in black. Black turtleneck, black slacks, black shoes, but no coat or jacket in sight. Dorie was in her skimpy shirt and a miniskirt and had on stilettos. I guess demons didn't feel inclement weather. In comparison, Adelaide, Adriana, and

I looked like roly-poly elves in our hat, scarf and heavy jacket-clothed bodies. I immediately started slipping on the icy road and again wondered how Dorie managed to sashay across the parking lot with nary a misstep.

I had one hand out just behind Adriana's elbow deferring to her pace, trying not to seem too apprehensive about her aged state and visions of a broken hip. I knew she'd clobber me if I even hinted that she might need assistance moving about, but I was ready to catch her just in case.

"Where is he? Where's my Antonio?"

Mortimer looked nervous and more than that—he looked scared. All this accomplished was making my insides begin to flip-flop and I felt queasy. Surely Mortimer could have gotten one centenarian out of a hole in the ground—unless it was a magic portal to another realm or something and we'd lost my great-grandfather forever.

"I'm not sure, but if I had to guess, I'd say he is somewhere in the prison either safe and sound—and we will have to admit to the Council we tampered in their business affairs to find the new entrance illegally—or he is at this very moment a prisoner of your renegade witch—or worse." Mortimer looked horrified as he uttered those words and I knew he was concerned that Adriana, at her age and despite being a feisty and powerful dark witch, would faint. She did look haggard, and I could see her physically trembling. I didn't think it was due to the weather.

"The minute he fell through, it sealed up tight. I tried everything I could think of to break the ward and remove the barrier, but nothing worked. It's as if the magic being used had no reversal spell, however, I do detect that only one kind of key—if you will—can release the ward and allow entry. Alas, I do not know what it may be, nor does that poor man have one on him. Either way, we need the assistance of the Council, because the man lying dead yonder did not die of natural causes as I suspected. He has been hit with some kind of death spell. I saw it fly through the air a second before it crashed into the poor fellow."

All eyes turned to the figure of the fallen man who did appear a rather intriguing shade of purple. Adriana ignored him and headed straight for the manhole. The ice that was now pelting us did nothing to deter her forward momentum.

"Whoa, there old lady! Hang on just a minute. You cannot blast a hole in the ground. You will get the entire family in trouble." I ran, slipping and sliding, over to Adriana just as she brought her magic up, fingertips sparking and cracking.

"Move it, Squirt. I mean business."

"I will not move. You have to listen to Mortimer."

"When have you ever known me to listen to anyone?"

"You can't do this. What if it's a trap? What if you blowing a hole in the ground causes harm to Grandfather Antonio? What if this is what Donna expects you to do?"

"Puleeze! How would she even know we chose this moment to follow a prison guard to this remote location and engineered this little farce?"

I reached my hand out and placed it on her outstretched arm.

"Because someone knew, how else do you explain that dead guy over there?" I jerked my head in the direction of the fallen man and felt Adriana relax her tense muscles, then lower her arms.

"You're right."

What? I never thought I'd hear those words come out of my great-grandmother, let alone having them be addressed to myself.

"I'm sorry. Can you repeat that? I don't think I caught what you said."

"Stop looking so surprised. The last thing I want to do is go off half-cocked and insane and have something I do result in something horrible happening to Antonio. Go sniff that body."

Hold up. See? And here I thought she was making sense and now I find the woman is madder than a monk whose spent his entire life talking to a tree stump on the top of a mountain.

"Sniff it? I am not sniffing a dead man! What is wrong with you?"

"Liliana, you are a Shadow Dancer. Go sniff that man and find out his secrets!"

The light bulb went off. "Do you mean like how I did with Gordon Delaney?"

Deputy Gordon Delaney was a former officer of the law here in Sweet Briar, Georgia. He was murdered and strung up on a tree outside the last magical location of the witch prison. The location was changed often, and the last one was in an abandoned Dairy Queen of all places. Gordon and I had never seen eye to eye and he'd made my life miserable whenever our paths crossed. You can imagine how upset I was when he turned up a ghost, haunting me for a tad, until Edith managed to convince him to move on. I'd owed my resident ghost big time for her intervention!

"No, dummy. I want you to tell me what kind of cologne he's wearing, if any. Of course I want you to do the same spellcasting you performed on Gordon!"

Well, she didn't have to call it sniffing!

"This will be the first time I do it without someone like Tanaquil helping me," I fussed. Tanaquil Alessi was an Elder in the Council of Witches and a friend. Her guidance was integral to my training since I had much to learn upon my return to my witch relations. The fact that I did not grow up knowing I was a witch was a major hindrance, yet Tanaquil always seemed to have faith in my abilities—I owed her much.

"You'll be fine. I have faith. I hope you brought your Oculus Rod." Adriana made shooing motions then crossed her arms, tapping her foot in impatience. That was the thing with my great-grandmother, she could rip you a new one at first, then perform an about-face, and build you up the next. As for the Oculus Rod—it was like my American Express Card—I never left home without it. Especially now that I knew I had stellar Shadow Dancer skills and was a rather superior Tracker.

I pulled the rod out of my bag and scrunched down next to the body. I didn't know if I should be concerned that I no longer felt a modicum of unease when faced with a stiff. I was more curious than anything as to what may have killed the man. I just hoped whoever did this to him had left behind a telltale trail of sorts.

Looking through the rod, I zoned out, closing down any outside distractions while I went up and down the length of his body. There was an icy thin layer of snow on him already, but that didn't stop me from noticing something odd about his countenance. Tiny bluish veins crisscrossed his skin, and I knew this is what probably gave him the purple appearance I'd noticed when we first arrived. There was a faint glow of yellowish amber, but thankfully I did not detect any green floating along with it. That is usually the harbinger that the person lying dead in front of me was about to sit up and begin a career in spooky hauntings. Green means ghost—don't believe me? Just watch Ghostbusters!

"Lorcan, reach into my bag and grab me a tiny vial, will you? I found something here."

After being handed a small glass bottle with a tiny cork stopper on the top, I managed to pop it open and use my magic to pull a sample while watching in satisfaction as the vial began to fill. Then I replaced the cork and put in in my pocket.

"We need to get this to Tanaquil so she can run tests, but I do believe this is the magic left behind by the attacker!"

"Brava, Liliana." Adriana smiled, albeit grimly. We were about to send out feelers to see if our witch sense could detect another entry to the prison, when we found ourselves surrounded on both sides by police vehicles. From the north came an SUV with an unknown person blocking the road to prevent anyone from coming upon us —or our trying to escape. From the south was the familiar cruiser that belonged to our sheriff, Glen Buford.

"Afternoon, folks. Care to tell me what y'all are up to?" Glen did not look amused to find the citizens of his town out of his jurisdiction and next to a dead man. I guess I can't blame him for the dark looks he was tossing at us.

"Antonio was at his cabin with Mortimer. They decided to go for a drive and found this body lying here." Adriana lied smoothly. "What I'd like to know, Sheriff, is what are you doing away from Sweet Briar and why is this officer blocking the way north? Isn't North Carolina about two more miles in that direction?"

Before Glen could respond, the door slamming on the SUV made us all jump, but none so much as Lorcan. He looked absolutely gobsmacked.

"Tiff? Is that you?"

"Oh my gosh! Lor! What are you doing here?" A

gorgeous blonde woman with long flowing locks came bounding over to us, not skidding once on the treacherous ice, despite wearing boots with heels. She threw herself into Lorcan's arms then proceeded to plant a loud kiss on his lips that she turned into a full on make out session in front of all of us. Lorcan didn't seem to realize he was returning the kiss.

Oh, hell no!

"Ahem."

"Where did you come from? I thought you moved to San Diego or someplace out west. Your mom said you entered the Marine Corp." Lorcan looking entirely enchanted by this leggy vixen, and completely ignored me clearing my throat. As a matter of fact, I think he temporarily forgot I existed. Since, when I tapped him on the shoulder, he glanced down at me with a frown of confusion, and it took him a good long pause for the fog to clear and realization dawn.

"Oh. Hey...uh, Lily. This is..."

"Lily! Is this the Lily Sweet I have been hearing all about? It must be, since I can't imagine there would be another Lily running around with such prominent citizens of Sweet Briar." The blonde police officer flicked her eyes to my family members, then gave me the once-over and smiled, yet it never reached her emerald-green eyes. She tilted her head to one side and placed her hand on Lorcan's chest. "Why, she is just the person I have been searching for. You see, we have received an anonymous tip that a renegade dark witch just murdered a man in cold blood. Then they named her, and wouldn't you know the name they provided me with was one, Lily Sweet of Sweet Briar?"

"And just who might you be?" Adelaide had found her voice and stared daggers into the smug officer whose continued fondling of my fiancé was making me madder than a hornet stuck on flypaper.

"Why, don't y'all recognize me? Other than the new deputy in town, I'm Tiffany Clarkson, of the Sweet Briar Clarkson's? After all, I went to school with Lorcan and Nora. We were all good friends. Until I went and broke them up and Lorcan here decided to date me instead of that tramp. Right, love?" Turning to gaze up at Lorcan and flash a smile that was all predatory, Tiffany then regarded me once more before dropping a bombshell that had me seeing red. "Not to mention that this fine man is my husband." This was emphasized by her running her hand to places on Lorcan's body no one other than me should ever deem proper to touch.

My magic crackled on and a bolt shot out of my fingertips before I could even think straight.

Bet you didn't see that coming. Or maybe you did.

Kind of like the left hook I managed to get in before all hell broke loose and I wound up in the back of the sheriff's cruiser with assault charges looming.

CHAPTER 4

"**I**'m going to kill that woman."

"Steady, Lily. Please stop saying such things in here." Jake Carter, my good friend and attorney, glanced around worriedly as I continued my grumbling and ravaged my long brown hair that now looked like a rat had nested in it.

"I don't care who hears me. I am going to kill that woman and enjoy doing it."

Groaning, Jake stood up and quickly shut the door closing off the rest of the police station from the room where I was locked up in the holding cell until things could be sorted and I could be released. Luckily for me, Tiffany had quick reflexes and my punch hadn't landed. I was in on a technicality and would soon be free. Then I was going to hunt down and kill that woman.

Jake was the son of my mom's and Aunt Jessica's best friend, June. June also happened to be the baby sister of Judge Owen Haywood, married to my Aunt Iona— Adelaide and Jessica's eldest sister, which made him my uncle. We liked to keep things close here in Sweet Briar.

Uncle Owen and Aunt Iona were the parents of the afore-mentioned Nora and my cousin Douglas. That Lorcan had one-time dated Nora still grated on my nerves. Now to find out he was supposedly married to this nasty blonde witch and furthermore, had lied to me? Lied to his family? Yeah. I was going to kill someone, and I might as well start with Tiffany Clarkson.

"Lily, Tiffany was just stirring up trouble as usual. To my knowledge, Lorcan has never married anyone. Heck he's barely dated, and Tiff has been away from Sweet Briar for years now. Why she decided to come back, and as our new deputy is beyond me. Don't let her get to you," Jake scolded.

Easy for him to say. He had a nice stable relationship with Becky Dolan, our town's bookstore owner and a sweetheart who would never have an ex pop up to cause trouble. I'm sure of it.

"Plus, you have worse things to worry about."

"Oh, really? Right now, I am the one sitting in a jail cell while that nasty woman is out there doing who knows what with Lorcan. He hasn't even tried to come back here to see me."

"Yes, he has."

"No, he has not."

"Lily. He tried, but Sheriff Glen isn't letting anyone but me back here and you are about to be released since they don't have much to hold you on. You are just lucky you've had a houseful of visitors to vouch for your whereabouts. Now we have to find out who tipped off the police and why they targeted you."

I rolled my eyes knowing I was doing a great impression of Adriana in the process, but I couldn't believe there was any doubt in anyone's mind who was behind all the drama around here.

"Seriously? Jake, come on! It is Donna and whoever she has aiding and abetting her! I don't have time for games right now. Grandpa Antonio is missing. He may be injured or worse, and this is a delay that could cost him and our family."

Jake was nodding his head in agreement, and I knew I shouldn't take out my frustration on him, but right now I wanted to punch someone, and she was in the next room, her voice trilling in a nauseating laugh.

"I am going to kill her. But first I am going to torture her."

Jake sighed and clasped my hands in his, trying very hard to get me to focus on him. I tried to pull my hands free, but he tightened his grip and gave them a little shake.

"Look at me. Lily, I mean it. You know this is total bull. We all do. The sheriff is well aware this is an attempt to sully your family once more. We just have to wait for the process and that means paperwork. Once the judge signs off on everything you will walk out of here, *out*, and not a word to Tiffany while you do. Then we can head over to your place to talk."

No sooner had Jake made this proclamation, then Glen Buford came strolling in looking upset yet determined. He unlocked my cell door, letting me out, but not before gripping my arm as I tried to pass him.

"Lily. Stay out of this. Do you hear me? We have the full report now and no one will suspect you of any foul play. We are trying to trace who made the anonymous tip by tracing the phone call in to the police station. Hopefully, it will lead up to the killer. Who else would call it in?"

"What about my great-grandfather?" I asked with trepidation.

"The Council is doing what the Council does best. Adriana is already there, tossing demands left and right. I know Olivia Ogden-Meyers and Tanaquil Alessi are with her. So have faith that mountains will be moved," he replied. "You are not out of trouble yet, however. That little display of magic might get you into trouble if my new deputy decides to file charges. And it won't be here at the police station, but with the Council. You need to reign in your temper, young lady."

"Sheriff Buford, about that. What can you tell me about this new deputy you hired? Why did she come back to Sweet Briar, and now? She is obviously one more in a long line of deputies I am going to have trouble with—I'm starting to get a complex!" Seriously, first Beau Buford, then Gordon Delaney, and now Tiffany Clarkson of the Sweet Briar Clarkson's, whatever the heck that meant.

"What about the dead man? I did a preliminary tracking spell on him. Any news yet?" I wasn't sure if Glen would answer me, and I saw his hesitation, but then he surprised both me and Jake by responding.

"He was a new hire, Orville Crawley. A minor witch who moved up from Florida to be with his aging aunt, Julia Crawley. She's one of Wilhelmina Dietrich's busybody friends, although no one deserves to lose a family member like that. The woman is a dragon, however. She gave poor Samantha Fairburn what for just because she was one minute late picking her precious nephew up from the airport. And Samantha was doing Julia a favor no less! That old bat." Glen paused, frowning at his tale, then rubbed the back of his neck wearily.

"I'm not making light of it. It's just that I've already heard an earful from that blasted family, and they are riling up a certain sector of the town who are aligned against your family. You can imagine how that is playing out right now. So, head home and lay low for a few days until I can sort this mess out. Please?"

I nodded my head.

"As for my deputy, she is from this town. Her family is prominent and also quite close to the Dietrich and Langsford clans. She is a highly-decorated veteran, so don't tell me I should have ignored her application. She has an admirable record, and I needed a deputy. I'm sorry for that little brush up, and I will have a talk with her, but this seems like something you and she—not to mention Lorcan, will need to work out. Don't cause any more trouble, got it?"

I nodded again, and pushed past the sheriff and into the main police station. Sitting on the other side of the barrier was Lorcan looking miserable, but not enough that he remained crestfallen. Instead, he kept tossing Tiffany the occasional smile while she regaled him with some story. He even laughed a bit—until he spied me heading in his direction. I didn't realize a man could turn so white without being a ghost.

Tiffany just gave me a knowing smile and flipped her platinum locks—that didn't look like they came out of a bottle, another reason to hate her—over her shoulder and parted her lips while raising one eyebrow. I knew a challenge when I saw one.

It wasn't until I waltzed past Lorcan, barely giving Tiffany a moment's glance and had reached the parking lot, that I realized Pandora was unaccounted for. I knew my mother had rushed off to gather reinforcements to aid in the Antonio recovery effort, Adriana was at the Council arguing her points, and Mortimer promised to remain behind and attend to the investigation—and hopefully be granted entrance to the prison in the process.

But what had happened to that pesky crossroads demon?

I didn't heed Lorcan's call as I rushed by in an effort to

escape committing a felony, but he decided to try my patience instead. I guess no one told him a tranquil Pisces is just a ploy to render an enemy clueless, and we usually went for poison if not outright gunfire. Or magic.

He'd learn.

"Lily, hold up, will you? Come on. Let me explain about Tiff."

Tiff, is it? No thanks, buster.

"Lily! Please stop. Let my drive you home at least. We can talk in private there."

Drive? All I had to do was continue to the corner, turn right then take the first left and go three houses in and I'd be home. I hardy needed a ride. I... hey! Where did they take my Jeep? If anyone so much as put a scratch on my new baby, there would be hell to pay! And I knew a demon and everything!

I heard Gordy Polk driving around the square in his garbage truck retrofitted into a plow and sander. The sound of salt hitting the roadway didn't do much to sooth my nerves, but at least I was grateful the sidewalks were cleared of the slippery stuff for the most part. There were still little patches of ice clinging precariously here and there. It made for slow going.

The air was chilly but humid. The ice had turned to sleet, and I wondered if we were going to get round two or if the weather would finally break, turning warm like it was supposed to be this time of the year. I looked up and could see I had witnesses watching my slow progress toward Main Street. Rita Chase was in the window of her store along with Samantha Fairburn, her assistant. June wasn't in her storefront, but Maureen Kennedy was. She gave me a double thumbs up then laughed. News traveled fast in this town and she was one of the townsfolk who wasn't my fan. That's ok; I disliked her as well.

I could hear Lorcan keeping up the pace behind me, not that my short legs could out-walk his long ones. I bet *Tiffany* could make long strides. What was she anyway? Five ten? Eleven? The freak. The tall, willowy, model-like freak. Lorcan was five eleven, for Heaven's sake! And he told me he liked short girls. Not that I'm short. I am five foot three, I'm still considered average.

"I do like short women—not that you're short or anything."

Gah!

Whenever I was frazzled, I was an easy target for mind reading among the witch community. Lorcan knew this and took a peek at my thoughts. Now I was really ticked off. I spun around and stood my ground as he almost barreled into me. Then I planted my index finger into his chest and poked him with every point I was making.

"One, I don't care who she is or what she meant to you. Husband! Really? You're married? I'd asked you before we got engaged after the whole "*Nora being on the banns*" thing if there was any other woman who would come out of the woodwork. You emphatically denied there was. Two, you let her kiss you and even reciprocated a little before you caught yourself which means there are still feelings there, and I am not one for sharing my man! Four, despite her denials which I am sure she's already fed you, that woman is hostile to me and is playing some kind of game even if she acts all innocent around you and says otherwise. I am not stupid. I know the games women play and that one is a champion player. I..."

"Three."

"What?" I frowned and ground my teeth together in frustration.

"You skipped three and went straight to four just now," Lorcan said quietly.

"I don't care about numbers! Don't try and distract me!" I stomped my foot and growled.

"Also, wasn't it you who I just found today rolling around in bed with another woman? If anyone should be upset, shouldn't it be me?" He said with a shrug and a little smile trying to lighten the mood with his words.

He did *not* just go there!

I stomped my foot and jabbed him even harder as I went on with my diatribe. "You have the gall to stand there and joke when my entire world is crashing down around me. I have a missing great-grandfather, a murder to solve —one that someone tried to frame me for—my family is frantic trying to end this attack on us and get my dad back, and now, on top of it all I have to bitch-slap your girlfriend —a wanton hussy who has taken it upon herself to move in on my fiancé—one who is about to have that title withdrawn. And she happens to be the new deputy! What is it with me and the deputies in this town?" I stopped poking Lorcan and rubbed my eyes. Exhaustion and fatigue were winning out over any further hostilities.

Lorcan took my momentary confusion as an invitation to get in my space and tried to hug me. He didn't stand a chance when I slugged him in his gut...hard. He wasn't expecting it, so he staggered backward and barely kept himself from going down on his backside. That is, until he reached out and grabbed onto my jacket. Then we both wound up on our backsides on the pavement. I could hear distant laughter and wasn't sure where it came from, but my guess was on Maureen.

Jake tried to run up to us, but in his haste, he managed to have his feet go out from under him and went airborne, landing in a heap on top of Lorcan. Great. Now *they* were nose-to-nose.

This time I could hear clapping.

I was adding Maureen to my murder list when Jake distracted me with his less than chivalrous actions. He gave Lorcan an apologetic smile and backed up, carefully standing. Then he held his hand out to help him to his feet, earning a menacing scowl from me. How dare he help Lorcan first, leaving me sprawled on the ground!

I managed to get up and dust off my jacket, ignoring Jake when he tried to help. I was about to continue my tirade, but it was at that moment Pandora chose to drive by.

In my Jeep.

She even waved as she flew past at breakneck speed.

What was worse, my cat, Wicked was riding shotgun. When the heck did she show up and why is she riding around in my Jeep with Pandora in an ice storm?

"I'm going to kill that demon."

"Which one?" Jake murmured.

CHAPTER 5

"I decide to sleep in one day and see all the excitement I miss?" My cousin, Andrea, huffed as she plopped down onto the sofa in my den. Wicked immediately jumped onto her lap and began to knead and purr—loudly. Her little zippy jaunt around the neighborhood in my Jeep didn't seem to have affected her adversely—not that I thought it would.

"Don't start. I can't believe it's still Saturday. I feel like I've been up for days."

My mother joined us after setting down a tray laden with three coffee mugs and a package of store-bought cookies. Hey! They were Knott's Berry Farm Boysenberry Shortbread cookies. They're incredible. I didn't need to have homemade all the time, not when I could savor these babies.

"Adriana is heading this way. She just called and informed me the Council plans on a formal inquiry into the death of Orville Crawley. You are a person of interest only because the Dietrich clan is making a stink along with the deceased's family. Although his aunt, Julia Crawley, wants an audience with you."

"What else is new? Well, Julia can get in line. How is Adriana getting here when her car is out of commission? And how did she get to the Council in the first place?"

I doctored my coffee and sat back, blowing into my mug to cool the brew.

"Tanaquil came to the sheriff's office and they left from there," Adelaide informed us. "But there is more, and it's not good. It looks like Donna was behind what can only be called a trap now. A ransom note showed up at the Council demanding her release in exchange for Antonio. The note is asking for a full pardon, a vehicle so she can leave Sweet Briar, and five hundred thousand in cash. The note says we have one week from today."

"Oh, this is horrible. I knew it. We need to do something now!"

"Lily. We need to wait for your grandmother to get here. We need to hear what the Council said, and Tanaquil. Without her wards strong enough for us to detect any shifter shenanigans, we are at a disadvantage. Having Lucretia trick us once was one time too many, you see. How can we trust anyone if we cannot tell if they are the real person, or an imposter? What if the next time we are told the location of the prison, and it is Gloria, or Olivia giving us the locale, it turns out to be yet another trick? Cool heads and a solid plan are what we need right now."

"But I'm worried about Grandpa Antonio. Why aren't the Council members doing more? Shouldn't they now have enough of a reason to let at least *all* of us inside to investigate? This is ridiculous!" I grumbled, taking too quick a sip then grimacing as I burned my tongue.

"Add an ice cube, silly. You're going to need that

tongue for when you have to eat crow and make up with your boyfriend," Pandora stated. She sat down cross-legged on the floor in front of the fireplace. I had the logs crackling away and Dorie was luxuriating in the warmth. Something about demons and hellfire and all the hotness she craves or some such.

"You hush. And give me back my Jeep key or we are going to tussle."

"Calm down, princess. I left it on the hook near the back door. You're such a drama queen!"

Andrea was a little shy around my new acquaintance and went wide-eyed at our bantering. I had to repeat several times first to her, and then my mom, what had tran-spired at the police station and my walk home. Andrea, of course, took up for Lorcan, as did Adelaide. I didn't want to hear it and held up my hand when they began to protest.

"Well, that was Glen. It looks like the Council gave him the OK to clear the body for the Soule's to work on. They are doing a full autopsy." Jake came in from the dining room where he was making phone calls on my behalf.

"I am not going there and dealing with those two. I don't care if Adriana breaks down and begs. I've already gotten the sample from the corpse," I stated.

"Don't worry, you don't need to do any more with your Shadow Dancing ability. I called Brian. He is on his way over and is taking over the case as lead detective even though he has his hands full with other cases," Jake finished.

"I better order pizza. What's up with Brian?"

"Oh, he has three or four cases going at once. Some-thing is going on with Shirley Jones, but he didn't share any info with me. Also, Rebecca Nightingale reported Rowan missing. Brian thinks she ran off with cousins from Atlanta because she was sick and tired of being stared at like a freak around here. Since she's legally an adult, there is not much he can do. But he has been diligently trying for Rebecca and Samantha Fairburn's sake. I think Samantha is paying him on the side in a private investigation capacity, so he doesn't give up the search."

"Why do I never find out these things yet everyone else seems to be in on the gossip? Who is coming over tonight?"

"Everyone. Well...unless you continue to have a frozen heart, everyone but Lorcan. Give the guy a chance to talk to you, Lily. Doesn't he deserve that at least?" Jake chided, hoping to shame me into forgiving Lorcan. "I can tell you Tiffany means nothing to him, and they were never married. I don't know what kind of game she is playing with that comment she made, but he is as single as I am. Don't you trust my word on it?"

"If you don't believe Jake, listen to me, Andrea added. I remember how relieved Lorcan was when Tiffany moved away. All she ever did was cause trouble. He had a bit of a crush on her but nothing more, and she blew it up to epic proportions and wound up ruining any chance Nora and Lorcan had of staying together. You should actually thank her for that!" I was not remotely interested in thanking that mongrel, despite her ruining the relationship between my cousin and Lorcan.

"Right now, my great-grandfather takes precedence. I don't have time for this drama! There is nothing to talk about. Lorcan lied to me about having another female love interest in his past, and he obviously still has feelings for Tiffany because he kissed her back!"

"What's this? Is the wedding off already?" Brian Chase, detective extraordinaire, and my sort of kind of ex, chose that moment to make his grand entrance. He turned to me, giving me a calculating look, then opened his arms and embraced me in a comforting hug. He may have held it a bit longer than necessary, and when Lorcan walked in not too far behind, I knew he'd planned it that way.

I felt the air crackling and knew Lorcan was upset. And because I wasn't one for playing games, all the ire whooshed out of me, and I turned toward my fiancé and gave him a level look.

"We are having pizza. Do you men want beer or soda? Or something else?"

Lorcan looked wary but relieved and knew we were heading for a talk when the time was right—namely when everyone was gone and we had the house to ourselves.

"Lily..."

"Don't. Not now. We can speak later."

"Here, sugar. Come sit by me." Dorie purred and tapped the seat next to hers.

Suddenly it all came crashing in and I knew I'd had enough.

"OK that's it. I am done with being nice. I am done with being teased. And I am most certainly finished with the crap that has befallen this household since before I was born. I am sick of a sluggish Council who is mired in red tape and bureaucracy. I am taking charge of this situation, and I don't want to hear a word of argument on the matter!"

"Well, well. It's about time you grew up and acted like the nastiest dark witch to come along in a century or two." In came Adriana, cloak flapping behind her like a bat's wings, nodding her approval at my little tirade.

What she didn't realize, nor anyone else in the room, was just how much I meant every word of it, especially since I knew something no one else present did. I'd split the sample from the crime scene into two separate vials and handed one over to Adriana to give to Tanaquil for testing.

However, I had already performed a preliminary test on it using my newly proficient skills in Shadow Dancing. What I discovered made my blood run cold but had me eagerly anticipating the outcome I was planning.

The magic I gathered at the crime scene was one-hundred-percent pure spellcasting by one Donna Fredricks. What was more, I had the skillset to link my magic with hers and when the time was just right, I fully intended on dropping in on my nemesis—with or without an army of my own.

"You can't be serious!" Adelaide cried frantically.

"I am most definitely serious," I replied.

"We have one week, and you are going to whip me into shape. Then I am going into the prison on the sly while the rest of you make noise and distractions galore. I am going to stomp that witch to oblivion while I find and free Grandpa Antonio."

But right now, none of us was going anywhere as the storm had intensified, and we looked to be stuck at my home for the time being. Brian and Jake stacked firewood near both fireplaces. Lorcan was making up spots for everyone to hunker down for the evening—even though he had a short walk through my back fence to reach his own place. I had a feeling if Jake and Brian were staying the night, so would he.

Tanaquil had dropped Adriana off and called to inform us she'd made it home safely before the storm worsened. So, it was just the men, Adriana, Andrea, and Pandora. Adelaide and I had some interesting company to help ride out this weather. As for Pandora, I didn't know if demons actually slept, so I wondered how this night would go. I had a feeling I would have to put wards around the *men* to keep her from messing with them. Becky had called to check on Jake and would be grateful to me for protecting his virtue, I'm sure.

Pizza consumed, we were all sitting around the dining room table strategizing. It seemed the only one who liked my idea was Adriana. No surprise there.

"I like it. With Tanaquil having completed the wards—and forty dedicated witches holding the magic needed to keep it in place round the clock, we no longer had to worry about being deceived by any evil shifters. Any who enter this town, live in this town, or drive through will have a soft white aura appear around their person until they are recorded, then be given a counter spell so they no longer glow. I've already had mine since I've trace amounts of shifter blood in me. And I've given Lily hers. It will be fun to see who starts glowing around town, although I doubt we have any others. With that taken care of, we can trust not having to worry about anyone deceiving us. Therefore, when Gloria gives us the new location of the prison, Lily can sneak inside and crush Donna."

"And how is she supposed to do that? It's not like Lily can walk in and not be detected, unless you have Andrea go with her and use her cloaking ability. But I suspect the wards at the prison will render that useless," Brian queried. His being a police detective didn't seem to be a hindrance to our plotting. Brian was firmly on my side and would gladly overlook my breaking and entering the prison it seemed.

"Leave that to me," I stated. "I have an idea."

"Care to share it with the group?" Lorcan decided to chance a question, and seeing as how I felt about him at the moment, it was rather brave of him, all things considered.

"No."

Andrea walked in with Dorie tailing her. Each of them had their hands full with coffee and a chocolate sheet cake.

"Where did that come from?" I asked.

"I brought it with me from my dad's café. Once I knew I was heading this way instead of going home, I figured why not cake?"

Why not cake indeed. Especially since her dad, my Uncle Stephen, made the best desserts around.

As we began passing around the coffee and cake, I couldn't help but notice my great-grandmother refusing either offering. I knew she must be frantic with worry over Antonio, and quite frankly, if I had to wager, I didn't like his odds one bit. Donna Fredricks is as evil as they come and insane to boot. Grandpa Antonio, while a powerful witch in his own right, is well over one hundred years old and frail. Plus, even if we gave in to her demands, she'd kill him anyway, I was sure of it. The news from the Council was bleak. When Antonio fell into that hole, he didn't wind up in the reception area of the prison. None of the workers saw him then or since.

That means Antonio must have been captured by Donna, and she had him as her prisoner.

I reached out my hand and placed it over hers giving it a little squeeze. When her gaze met mine, the pain there almost did me in. No way was I going to let my great-grandparents' love affair end at the hands of a demonic witch on a mission of hate and devastation. Not on my watch.

"Grandmother, why do you think Lucretia worked with Donna in the first place. Have you looked into the family line? Why did she hold such hate for the family? And did you know there was shifter blood in our line?"

"Lucretia Dolce was from an ancient and powerful

witch dynasty, and married a Romano, from another venerable family, but was in love with a village boy of no pedigree," Adriana began. "The family documents state he may not have even had powers. His family was recorded in the books which means there were witchfolk in the line, but they were so low in the annals to be deemed unworthy as far as the Dolces were concerned. That the Dolce and Romano clans often married, even distant cousins, belied their desire to keep the strength in the bloodlines. I am connected to Antonio not only by marriage, but we are cousins in some convoluted ancestral tree that I haven't bothered to trace. Lucretia's father forced her to marry a Romano and threatened the family of the village boy should the lad interfere." Adriana sat back and folded her hands on her lap.

"So, all this is a vendetta of sorts because she wasn't allowed to marry a village boy? Isn't that a bit extreme even for witches?" I wondered aloud.

"It might be considered extreme until you hear the rest of the story. I almost feel bad for the woman after what I discovered but not quite. After all, it was she who killed my grandfather Marcus' wife, Amelia." Adriana said, looking sorrowful before she continued. "However, her tale of woe is just as horrid, and I wonder if that is what made her so evil. What Lucretia never informed her parents was that she was with child. They forced her to give up the baby to the young man's family, concealing the fact from the public. Then after the baby was taken away, she was forced to marry Rodolpho Romano. Her new groom took it upon himself to seek out his young rival and force him into a duel. After Rodolfo confronted the young man, he said something ungentlemanly about his new bride, causing the young man to lash out, striking him in the face. This lad was a humble cobbler, had never dueled a day in his life, he didn't even know how to use a weapon. Rodolpho knew a magical duel would not be approved by any court in Rome, so he chose swords. It was over before it even started."

We sat in silence and thought Adriana had completed the dark tale, but then she began to speak once more.

"Rodolpho drained his rival of all his blood and returned to his castle where he had all his minions perform the blackest magic with his victim's blood. A horror-stricken Lucretia begged her husband to stop such revolting magic and let her young man rest in peace. Instead, Rodolpho cursed the blood and created atrocities in his name. What is worse, Antonio's father, being a cousin of Lucretia's father, forced the family of the young suitor to give up their trade and move away to an undisclosed location, effectively preventing Lucretia from ever seeing her child or knowing what became of it. Lucretia swore that day that she would end the Dolce and Romano line and avenge her beloved. Lucretia is my direct descendant but is related to Antonio as well. You can see why our family was attractive to her as a target."

It was indeed a dark tale and made me question being loyal to my own family after hearing such atrocities. However, I also knew the sins of the father, or mothers, could not be held on the heads of their offspring. Grandpa Antonio certainly was a fine example of a loving and generous man. He is nothing like his own misguided father.

"I can see why Donna and Deanna, being illegitimate Croys, were such attractive allies for someone like Lucretia. What better way to destroy a family she despises than by aligning oneself to another family who hates just as strongly as she did?" Adelaide said.

I agreed with her, as did everyone in the room. We were a somber group pondering all we'd just been told. It was a tragic story.

"The shifter magic comes from the Romano side, I believe. Antonio looked deeply into his family record and found no mention of such. But my Romano side held family secrets, and the fact that we have shifter blood could very well be one such enigma that was lost over time."

"Will it manifest in us—me?" I worried. After all, I now have not only *witch* blood, but siren and shifter in me. I was effectively a paranormal mutt of some substance.

"I believe it is a latent gene. It is there but not manifesting and probably weak, unlike your siren blood. This is one of the reasons the various families coveted the pure blood lines so as not to muddy the waters with the unknown outcome of mixing Breed. Only time will tell what will come of all this," Adriana informed us. "Plus, you aren't glowing. So, I doubt it's strong in you. Better to take the potion anyway, just in case."

"It's like my sister, Iona. She has no siren abilities, nor did Jessica. Only I have it—and through me, Lily." Adelaide stated. "It worries me, however, because Lily doesn't know how to control the siren power in her, not that I think it weakens you dear, however, if you don't learn how to master it you will have adverse effects."

"Like what?" Great. Just what I needed. More issues!

"You are more likely to pass out when agitated or upset, because your siren magic is vying for control along with your witch power. This causes a short circuit, if you will, and it can create a lack of oxygen in the brain."

"That's why I've been hitting the deck so often! I was starting to worry that something might be wrong with me. But how do I learn how to control the siren side of me?"

"You have the sweet briar rose jewelry now, and their powers will strengthen the more you wear each item—but those aid your witch side. I see you never take the briar ring off the index finder of your right hand. You need to find Tarni again. Tell her you are aware of your siren blood and see if she will give you a boon— a talisman or jewel, that you can use to channel the siren side. Better if it is infused with her tears. Maybe another ring to wear on your right hand. I do not know if she will grant this request, but she is the only one I know of who can help you. I have one such item, but it was given to me for that very reason, and alas, I cannot let you have it, darling."

"I have the jewelry Jessica left for me as well. But much of that, with the exception of the family ring, was stuff my dad got for me when I was little, and I assume you did as well?"

Adelaide nodded yes and I began to consider everything I'd just learned. I wondered if Tarni was still at Nichols Pond and could survive in such frigid waters. I knew nothing about the lore surrounding sirens and my attempts at interrogation did nothing but confuse me and amuse her to no end. I was quickly and succinctly informed that, no, sirens did not sport long shiny tails. Would Tarni gift me with something so precious?

It didn't escape my notice that while we discussed all these things, Pandora kept an enigmatic look on her face, like she knew something the rest of us didn't. I wanted to question her further about her intentions and why she chose now to show up because I didn't believe in coincidence, but I chose to wait until I could corner her alone and drill her for the answers I sought. Something told me not to put her on the spot.

"Would you look at that?" Jake suddenly spoke up, looking at his phone in amazement.

"What's wrong?"

"Nothing's wrong, but if this weather forecast is accurate, tonight's storm will be over by midday tomorrow then we are heading for a warming trend. And I mean, a serious warming trend. By Tuesday, we might reach temperatures in the sixties!"

Andrea sat up from her sprawled position on the sofa in the formal living room where she'd been lounging. "Sixties! That is positively balmy! I don't get this weather at all."

"Yeah, well it looks like we are going from ice storm to tornado warnings in a matter of days!" Jake replied.

Oh, fun. I hadn't yet experienced anything like tornado warnings yet since living in the south. This should be great.

"The warming trend is good for one thing," Adriana proclaimed.

"What's that?" I asked.

"It will give you and Adelaide a chance to spar and hone your fighting skills before we have to battle Donna at week's end. Rain or shine, tornadoes or not, you two will be outside preparing for battle."

Now *that* was something I could get behind.

Well, minus the tornadoes of course!

CHAPTER 6

By Tuesday morning, the weather had indeed turned warmer. Not the sixties as predicted, but I'd take fifty-five degrees over the freezing sleet and icy mess we'd had for the last week or so. Even the air smelled of spring and I couldn't believe how quickly Mother Nature could change her mind around these parts!

That's one of the reason why I was in town, on the square, when a thin blade flew past my head before I could duck. Five more came flying by in rapid succession and I managed to avoid getting impaled by all of them.

No, I wasn't under attack.

Well, technically that isn't true. I was being attacked, but not by an enemy. Adelaide spent the better part of the morning training me on the finer points of knife throwing. Tactical maneuvering and the best usage for such magical tools I now had at my disposal. Throwing knives, darts, daggers, you name it, I was getting one heck of a crash course in all things sharp and deadly. I just couldn't believe how much I was enjoying it.

"Missed me again!" I laughed and I hit the ground

rolling then spun back to my feet tossing a ball of energy directly at my mother's face. She easily sidestepped the attack, but Stu Jones wasn't so lucky. He got clobbered head-on when he walked out of the pharmacy and headed toward Joe's Diner.

"Oops! Sorry, Mr. Mayor! Just give it a few minutes and those warts will go away!"

Adelaide and I were doubled over laughing at the mischief we were causing. More than one business owner had come out to watch our tomfoolery but quickly ran inside when they, too, became near-victims. I wasn't used to having my magic be on public display, but our tourist season didn't start until April, and the town was pretty much still locals only.

The bus load of Baptists notwithstanding.

They were just passing through heading over to Hiawassee. I doubt they'll even remember me levitating Maureen Kennedy so high up in the air that everyone and their brother caught a glimpse at her worn out knickers!

Hey! I put her down.

Eventually.

Thankfully, we had Andrea standing guard, and she quickly sent a stream of *"forget what you've seen here folks,"* magic at them.

"Try hitting me with the stun spell again."

I'd been practicing that one for weeks but for some reason I couldn't seem to get it to work. I called it the *truth serum stunner*. When performed properly, it rendered your victim motionless yet able to speak, with the added caveat that they were also unable to lie to you. A handy trick and one I intended to master—someday. The last time I'd tried to hit Adelaide, it bounced off of her and slammed into an old lady walking her dog. The dog wound up at Doc Holcomb's and I wound up with the bill.

My mother was a decent seamstress and had taken my measurements so she could procure me what she deemed, "a proper fighting ensemble." I had clothing on that no big chain store or even mom-and-pop shop in these parts would ever dream of carrying. Maybe in a costume shop or at some cosplay event, but my pants, top, boots, gloves, and belt all were crafted with one thing in mind—freedom of movement and the ability to toss spells with abandon. And when that didn't work, allow easy access to any number of ordinary weaponry on my person. I felt like a ninja. Or Lara Croft.

I was having the time of my life.

Everything I wore was in varying shades of browns and greys. Better to blend in and not get noticed, or so said Adelaide. The fabric is indescribable but something akin to suede and leather, with mesh insets and plenty of loops and zippers to attach weapons or tuck them away for safe-keeping. My gloves were incredibly soft yet had amazing grip. The tips of my fingers were exposed so my magic would not be blocked. My top was formfitting and had secret pockets that allowed me to carry vials and powders that I could use to enhance any spell or armament in my arsenal.

"Ok. Enough playing. Let's try hand-to-hand combat and some weapon moves. I know most of your fighting will be of the magical variety, but you need to know the basics and you need to be quick and decisive once you find your-self up close and personal with someone."

Adelaide and I spent the next two hours going through her repertoire of fighting skills. We did various maneuvers until she seemed satisfied with me. Who knew those free *taekwondo* lessons I took as a kid would come in handy?

The last skill we worked on for the day was my least favorite. At least in the sense that I couldn't imagine any scenario ever where I would need to use this particular skill set. Swordplay. Or sword fighting, if you will, since I'd doubt I'd be playing if and when I ever used it.

Not only did I have a kickass outfit to wear, but I also had an amazing arsenal of material to hold my various weapons close to my body. The sheath that held my sword was strapped to my back yet felt lightweight and nonexistent. The perks of having magic along for the ride. Another perk was that the sword was enchanted, and once I slipped it back in the scabbard, it shrunk to a nonexistent appearance. Looking at my back, you'd see buckles and straps and material, but certainly not a long, thin sword poking out!

Adelaide taught me how to clear the sword from the leather scabbard in one easy movement, how to properly hold it, and the different movements and methods of attack. Over and over we mock-battled until I felt a tiny bit of confidence creep into my soul that maybe I could actually put up a decent fight should I ever have the need.

By the time we had finished, both of us were sweating and starving. That meant one thing. Towel off and head to Joe's for some well-deserved food!

"You two ladies had every male within six miles of town transfixed on your little show of strength and agility earlier. My goodness! But you two were a sight!" Sheila Polk, waitress and friend, proclaimed as we took our seats in my favorite booth. "What can I get you?"

"Sweet tea, please!" The official drink of the south had finally won me over, and I couldn't' imagine my life without it any longer. Andrea and I both opted for that, but Adelaide declined asking only for water with ice.

"You are looking well, Adelaide. Being out of that kitty prison suits you!" Sheila gave my mom a hug before she, too, could take her seat across from me in the booth.

"Thank you, Sheila. It certainly feels good being me again, although every once in a while I get a hankering for some catnip." Both women laughed and Sheila went off to get our drinks while we took some time to peruse the menu.

"I don't know about you, but all that exercise has made me one hungry girl. I think I'm going for a juicy burger, fries, and a chocolate malt. What about you two?" I asked as Adelaide closed her menu and sat back regarding me.

"I'm in," Andrea said, grinning in anticipation.

"Sounds good to me. Lily, have you spoken with Adriana since Saturday? I've tried to call her but am having no luck reaching her."

I frowned at this news and thought back on any attempts I made at reaching my great-grandmother. "I think we briefly spoke Sunday morning when she made it home from my place. Now you have me worried because I know all of her focus is on Grandpa Antonio. She has to be a total wreck not knowing how he is and even more so, how he's being treated. I'm anxious myself."

All the jocularity of the last few hours ebbed away as I was reminded of the seriousness of what my great-grand-father might be going through while we sat here enjoying lunch. I hope they were feeding him and keeping him warm and comfortable. Or were those working with Donna so vile it was already too late, and Antonio was dead? I couldn't bring myself to believe he might be gone forever so I focused on what I needed to do right now to hopefully bring him home safely.

"I'm going to get into that prison one way or another."

"I know you are."

"Just so you know, even though we planned on sneaking me in somehow, but if the distractions fail, if the Council refuses us entry, I will be getting in that place if I have to get arrested to do so." Hey, now. That wasn't such a bad idea. What better way to get into the very place I'd been trying for so long to gain entry, than to get myself into some kind of trouble that would have me incarcerated in the very place I needed to be.

"What are you thinking, Lily? I see those wheels turning," Andrea asked and she began to worry her napkin.

"I'm thinking that if I can't get in one way, another option might be to do something that would result in having me tossed in the prison—nothing too nefarious. After all, I'd like to come back out again. However, what if I do something to upset the Council enough that they have no option but to put me in prison for a week or two? The thing is, just what do I do that will allow that to happen?"

"Are you crazy? Lily! You are taking a huge risk by putting yourself at the mercy of the Council. Not everyone on it sides with our family! Don't forget that the Dietrichs and the Langsfords want any reason they can find to have the Dolces knocked down so far that they will never recover. Then their side becomes the power players in this town and beyond." Andrea finished her diatribe and drank down half her tea just as Sheila came up with our meal.

"Here you go, ladies. I'll be right back to refill your drinks."

I watched Sheila head to the back of the diner where the new waitress whose name I never could seem to remember was waiting on Stu and a buddy of his. The warts were indeed gone—on Stu—I have no idea if his friend has warts.

"Hey, ladies. Nice to see your smiling faces. Burgers good?" Joe, the chef par excellence and owner of the diner that bore his name, poked his head out of the kitchen to greet us. "You are looking particularly wicked, Lily. I like that getup you are wearing!"

"It's my new kick-butt/dark-witch look. I think it suits me."

"It does indeed. Now you just have to find someone to rough up a little. Need a volunteer?"

Laughing at Joe's offer, my thoughts returned to the task at hand.

I knew my family would give me trouble on this plan I'd cooked up, but I couldn't see how else to get into the prison unless someone like Mortimer could bust a hole into the side. My mind went to the newest paranormal to come uninvited into my world. Perhaps Pandora could be of use here. After all, she showed up just as all this went down. Wait a minute! What if she is playing both sides? Whoa. What if she is working with Donna?

"We need to hurry up. I have to go find Dorie and have a little talk with her."

"What's wrong, Lily? Your face ran a gamut of emotions on it just now. What gives?" Andrea asked.

"Listen up. I have a few questions I need to run by that creature, and I put it off way too long. She has been in and out and Heaven knows where since she showed up on Saturday, and I need to know where she stands. I know you had a rather simpatico relationship with her in book form, Mom, but I don't like this crossroads demon business. I need to know what game she's playing—if she is playing one."

"I can assure you she was benign when we were young. I don't see why she would suddenly morph into something we need be concerned with, dear. Although she did tend to lead me into mischief. But I can see you are determined to track her down and have words. Tread lightly, however. Crossroad demons are powerful beings—demigods— ancient and incredibly unreliable. Pandora has been

around for a long time, despite her looking like a recalci-
trant teenager who got into her older sister's closet."

She did have a point, but I still needed answers and a
strong ally. I had to know where Pandora stood, and I
needed to know it now.

CHAPTER 7

I was all set out to head directly home and confront Pandora, or search for her until I could. But when I left Adelaide and Andrea at the diner, I ran into someone who looked so out of character in their distress, it left me no choice but to stop and inquire into their well-being.

"Shirley? Is everything ok?"

Shirley Jones looked anything *but* ok. Our usual jolly and over-the-top EMT wore no makeup. Her hair—a customary bouffant straight out of the fifties—was flat and dull. I barely recognized her and wouldn't have if she hadn't been in uniform.

Startled, Shirley jerked her head up and looked confused for a fraction of a second, and what's worse, she looked scared. "Oh, Lily. Hi. How are you?"

What—no hon, doll, or toots? This subdued character was so far away from the vivacious and lively woman I knew and loved that all thoughts of finding Pandora flew out the proverbial window. At least until I could solve this mystery.

"I'm fine, but how are you? Is anything wrong?"

"Lily, what isn't? I don't know what to do, who to talk to, or where to turn! I'm going crazy with worry!"

"Whoa! Slow down. Tell me what happened. Maybe I can help?"

"But that's just it, Lily! No one can help! No one!"

And with that, Shirley hopped into her ambulance and drove off. In her haste to leave, two of the wheels hopped the curb then she righted her vehicle and sped off toward the south side of town. What of earth is going on with Shirley? I knew Brian was looking into whatever was wrong, but I still felt concern after seeing her like this. I almost turned back to confront Sheila or Stu since they were both her siblings and in the diner, but at that moment I spied the very demon I'd been hoping to find. What's more, my cat, Wicked, was with her.

I'd have to put off what was ailing Shirley until a later date.

Crossing the street at a fast clip, I managed to reach the door to June's Emporium just behind Pandora who'd already entered. June's Emporium was the pride and joy of June Carter, Jake's mom. The proprietress was behind the counter having a lively conversation with a customer shopping for cauldrons and didn't see me at first. Dorie was looking at a row of wands and crystal balls which were on the same aisle as the toasters and hair dryers. June's place had a mixture of magical and mundane in a hodgepodge of wonderfulness so tourist and townsfolk alike couldn't stay away very long.

The tourists bought into the whole *folksy, witchy, RenFest,* vibe our town was famous for. The townsfolk knew better.

I sidled up to Pandora, keeping one eye on Wicked who was stalking an unsuspecting Maureen, dusting the shelves on the far wall. I knew what was coming but didn't have the heart to stop my inky black feline from having a bit of fun. Anyone but Maureen Kennedy and I would have stopped her. I was just jealous she could get away with torture while I couldn't. Therefore, living vicariously through my cat was the only option.

"What is going on? Why are you out and about and with my cat?" I whispered furiously trying to keep my voice at a level that would neither disturb June, nor make Maureen aware of her impending doom.

Especially since her impending doom was now doing that cat butt wiggle-wiggle, all evil beasties do just before pouncing.

"Can't a girl shop?"

"You aren't a girl, and I didn't know demons needed much in the way of housewares, or witchy trinkets."

"I'm a girl. Last I checked I didn't have a third leg or anything like that!"

"You know what I mean. You are an ancient being who can probably make this town go up in a puff of smoke or something equally distressing. What I'd like to know is why you have now decided to come out of that book and..."

"Arrgh! Get it off me! Get it off me! Help!"

"Wait here."

I casually walked around the counter to where Maureen was spinning in a circle, shrieking, trying to remove my demon child who was firmly attached to her scalp. Every twist and turn had Wicked digging her claws in deeper and lashing her tail like a whip. Occasionally she'd take a nip on the tip of Maureen's ear or the top of her head.

"Come on, you. Playtime is over." Snapping my fingers, and tapping my foot was all it took to have Wicked break her maniacal hold on Maureen, and nonchalantly jump onto the counter near a frazzled June and her wary customer. She began to wash and purr. I know my mother was glad to be out of her feline prison, but times like these had me wishing I could merge with her if just for a few hours.

"That cat needs to be put down. It's a menace to society. It probably has rabies!" Maureen screeched.

"Well, I definitely need to bring her to the vet now. Heaven knows what kind of social disease you are carrying that might transfer to her."

"You are crazy. Your entire family is nuts. All of you. Especially that old bat of a grandmother of yours and your shameless mother."

I felt a whisper of my magic stir, wanting to be let out to play as my eyes turned to slits. Impugn me all day long. Talk about my family, especially my newfound mother, and heads were going to roll. I kept it under control, however. Maureen wasn't worth the trouble.

"Maureen. Take yourself to the back room and go clean up. Lily, please take Wicked outside. This is a place of business!" June scolded.

A red-faced Maureen flounced out of the shop heading to the kitchen while an amused Wicked tracked her departure. One would think June would have me toss my cat to the street, but one look at the woman now stroking the length of my furball gave me all the proof I needed that Maureen was finally getting on June's nerves as well. She had been rather lenient when it came to the town bully, and I think Maureen's days of doing not much more that pass a rag around haphazardly were numbered.

Hey, you get what you deserve. And Maureen deserves as much naughtiness as I can throw at her and then some.

"What's with the cow-faced slug?" Dorie asked, jerking her head toward the kitchen.

"That girl has been a thorn in my side ever since I

returned to Sweet Briar. I was always nice to her, but she disliked me from the minute she met me and now all bets are off. Plus, she was the town bully during her high school years and terrorized many of her peers. I've decided to be her Karma. So has Wicked. It's all for a good cause."

"To drive her mentally unstable?"

"Got it in one."

Pandora chuckled and then looked inquiringly at June who'd finished with her customer and had walked over to where we were standing.

"As much as I adore this beautiful puss, puss. I must insist you keep her from terrorizing Maureen. This is the third time in as many weeks!"

"What? I had no idea Wicked was coming in here and attacking Maureen, June. This is the first I'm hearing about it."

June sighed and gave my cat another fond pat. "Well, I didn't want her to get into trouble. But honestly, Lily. I can't have her coming in here and causing such a ruckus! Last Tuesday, she cornered Maureen in the stockroom, and I lost four brand new crystal balls! Glass and smoke and magic sparking everywhere. It was a mess!" June lamented.

"Oh, no! I promise I will make good on those damaged items. You should have called me."

June glanced at Pandora and frowned slightly, then turned on her shop owner smile. "Forgive my manners, may I help you find something?"

"Sure, sugar. I need a hunting knife and a rope. A good sturdy one."

June nervously tittered then realized Pandora was serious. "Oh, um, I have some knives. But they are more ritual athame knives, not hunting ones. My husband, Dennis, he has a hardware shop next door and could accommodate you with a hunting knife and some rope."

"Do you have a heavy-duty blender?" Pandora asked, grinning, and showing all her teeth.

Blinking in confusion, June cleared her throat and nodded yes, then pointed to a display shelf in the corner. "I have an excellent one right over here. It can crush ice, blend, and chop just about anything you throw at it."

"Guts, even, I wonder?" Pandora mused to herself, tapping her fingers to her lower lip. I wanted to kick her for being such an imp.

"Um, well, I guess."

"I'll take it then!" Clapping like a little girl whose dad just brought home a pony, Pandora sauntered over to the register and pointed at me with a knowing grin on her face.

"Just bill Lily here and send the package to her house. She owes me one. Only she has no idea why yet!"

&.

"I owe you one. Really? Do you care to explain or am I supposed to begin guessing what you mean by that?"

"Don't be silly. If I told you right now, I'd have to kill you. Hey! Is that a café? Let's head over. I want something sinfully delicious. Get it? Sinful?"

Before we could head into the direction of my uncle's café, we spied Brian Chase exiting his car across the street from us. He paused when he noticed us.

"That's your super-hot ex isn't it?" Pandora purred.

"Dorie, not now."

"Ladies. Lily, I'm glad I ran into you. I've got some information for you to pass on to Adriana. That manhole cover was definitely tampered with. It was requested as a new entrance by the Council, only Gloria had no idea Orville Crawley was even assigned as the new warden yet, nor that north of Tate City would be the new location. Someone got to him before she was informed, and he probably followed whoever set this up's directions. He was tricked."

"What does that mean, exactly?" I asked.

"It means someone suspected your family might be trying to find a way into the prison and dangled Orville as a sacrificial lamb, then made sure the new entry point turned into a trap. Someone on the outside is helping Donna on the inside still. We have a highly worrisome situation because it could be almost anyone."

"Who would have known Mortimer and Antonio were at the cabin and planned on tracking Orville?"

"That's the question of the hour, now isn't it? Look, I have to run. I'm buried in paperwork, but I will try to stay in touch."

"I just saw Shirley. She looked awful. Is everything OK with her, or is she in some kind of trouble?"

"I can't talk about that right now, Lily. But I'm on it."

I thanked him and snapped my fingers at Pandora who suddenly came down with a case of roving hands, much to my dismay and Brian's surprise.

"Oops. Sorry. I was born this way."

"Somehow I don't think that has anything to do with why you had your hand on his behind, Dorie."

"It's a nice behind."

"That's beside the point."

Brian scurried away looking a bit dazed, and I swung my eyes to Pandora who was tossing her hair behind one shoulder and licking her lips like Brian was a lamb chop and she was starving.

"Quit it."

"What? I can look. And nibble."

"Forget that kind of nibble and let's go over to the café before you get arrested."

Running across the street on stilettos that had to be at minimum five inches, Pandora stopped traffic in both directions. It didn't help that the wind kept whipping her miniskirt up over her hips giving everyone a flash of red panties. That she was even wearing such a skimpy outfit in this weather would have garnered those looks alone. But the white miniskirt and matching fuzzy tight sweater which showed off her perfect body was just the beginning. Those red stilettos drew the eye down long, long legs and the matching red bows in her blonde pigtails completed the overall naughty schoolgirl look to perfection.

Gordy Polk was sitting in his garbage truck, mouth open in amazement.

Donald Murphy stopped short on the opposite side of the road but still managed to tap the bumper of Dev Patel, the veterinary assistant on his way to work. Even the good and God-fearing Reverend Oliver Brewster came screeching to a halt, mouth agape, and stared long enough for unholy thoughts to cross that narrow mind of his, I'm sure. That is until the equally God-fearing spouse, the ever dour Laura Brewster, slugged him with her purse and they continued on their way. And I already knew Brian left us a bit on the shell-shocked side.

The woman was a menace.

I can't imagine what Dorie wore in the dead of summer. I shuddered at the thought of the destruction that would rein down on the town and its citizens should she show up in an itsy-bitsy little bikini.

Ding! Went the little bell on the door of my Uncle Stephen's café. And that was the last sound anyone heard since all chatter stopped. That is, until my cousin, Steve Junior walked in carrying a tray of eclairs.

"Be still my heart, it's the woman of my dreams if only she weren't marrying a grease monkey with big brown eyes. What can I do you for, Lily?" Steve winked and threw out a laugh, then began to choke and cough when his eyes landed on Dorie.

Steve was rendered speechless.

You have to understand just how incomprehensible this was to me. Steve *never* had a loss of words flowing out of his self-assured and mildly egotistical mouth. Ever. Like, *ever*.

"What do we have here? Is every man in this town a scrumptious cupcake or am I in heaven? Oh! I made a funny! Me, talking about heaven!" Dorie batted her lashes and leaned across the bar to sniff at the eclairs that were threatening to slide off the tray Steve was holding haphazardly.

The murmuring began when Uncle Stephen poked his head in and yelled at his son to get a move on. He didn't even give a second glance to Pandora, but he did wink at me. When a man was married to someone as incredible as my Aunt Chiara, another gorgeous creature didn't register, I guess. Either that, or he was a master at hiding his emotions! The poor lad who worked the counter, a shock of red hair and freckles galore—not to mention Maureen's beau—Tommy the gormless, just stood rooted in one spot practically drooling.

"I want two of those yummy looking things you are holding. Oh! And two of these, what are they called? Napoleons? Ha! You people named a treat for little Leo? He was such a tyrant! Ah, the fun times we had. You know what? Give me two of everything in the case. I'm starving."

Steve would need two of their biggest boxes to be able to fit all the treats Dorie asked for. And just who did she think would carry them back to my place? Not to mention, where did she put everything she stuffed in that svelte frame of hers? Every woman in the place was staring daggers at the demon, not that she was paying it any mind. That is, until one diner in particular made herself known.

"What have we here? Have you decided to go slumming, Lily? Where did you find this character? Down on Fulton Industrial Boulevard on a weeknight?" Cousin Nora snickered, giving Pandora the once-over.

"No, love, I erroneously asked your pimp where you shopped, and he let me go through your closet. I think I have scabies now."

Whoa.

Even Nora looked shocked. I don't think anyone ever had a comeback as fast and devastating as that one. Not to Nora. Not ever.

"Listen, you skank. I come from a prominent family and have a pedigree that far surpasses anything you can toss out of your foul mouth. Obviously your breeding is lacking. I'm surprised you are hanging with mongrels now, Lily."

"Yet you are licking the boots of a rival family and making a laughingstock of yourself with your fetching and curtsying like hired help. My how far _you've_ fallen, dearie. Now move away; the smell of manure is ruining my appetite."

Nora blinked. She opened and closed her mouth a few times then growled.

"You aren't even worth my time."

"That's what your last john said. Now run along. I'm bored." Pandora turned back to Steve and all but dismissed my cousin.

Nora knew a lost battle when she saw one and rushed out of the café, albeit with her head held high and shoulders back. I had a feeling I would be the one to pay for that lovely little exchange.

"Now, who is going to carry these boxes back to Lily's home? I'm ready to pig out!"

Steve all but jumped over the counter, tossing his apron at Tommy.

"Take over kid, I've got a job to do. Let's go ladies. The last one home has to feed me a cannoli."

I think we all could guess just who that would be.

CHAPTER 8

"You ate two entire boxes of pastries. How did you eat two entire boxes of pastries without throwing up?"

"I have a good constitution. That was an awesome treat, but what's for dinner tonight?" Pandora queried.

I was holding my stomach and groaning. The effort to sit upright was too much for me so I remained in a semi-reclined position on the sofa in my den. Pandora was flitting around the room looking at photos on the mantle and picking up knickknacks then setting them down again. Her frenetic pace was making me nauseous. I had two cannoli, one napoleon, and a baba. An incredible number of sweets in one sitting. Dorie had five times that amount and was still nibbling on the last of the pastries, wondering what we were having for dinner.

I can't even.

"Too bad that Steve guy couldn't stay long. He's way hot."

"Pandora, Dorie, listen. We need to talk."

"No good outcome ever came by someone starting a

dialogue with "we need to talk," so I'm thinking you are worried about my intentions. Am I right?"

"My mother vouched for you, but I need more than how nice you were to my parents and Aunt Jessica when they were children. I need to know why you are here now. Why were you in book form, why come out now? And just what is a crossroads demon, anyway?"

Twirling in place then plopping into one of my comfy chairs, Dorie tucked her feet up under her bottom and settled back, preparing for what turned out to be an enlightening conversation in more ways than one.

"A crossroads demon is just what it sounds like. We work the crossroads at midnight, waiting for troubled souls who are willing to bargain for a better life. It's the afterlife they need to worry about, only they either don't realize this or don't care at the time. Life has run these folks to the ground, and they would willingly give up their souls for a nice go-around in the wheel of life."

"That's horrible. You take advantage of the downtrodden." I was trying not to judge, but I couldn't get my head around thinking it was good practice to sell your soul to a demon when you were down and out on your luck. I'm sure every crossroads demon out there made the bargain sound like an incredible opportunity—kind of like a military recruitment officer. They promise the world until they nab you, then the reality of your situation sets in, but it's too late.

"Got it in one, sister."

"You read my mind! But I was blocking!"

"Lily, Lily, Lily. It is not about blocking. It's about deflecting the intrusion and implanting another thought in the mind of those that seek entry. You were taught the basics since you've been back, but you never had the advantage of growing up witch. You are having trouble keeping people out of your head because you have multiple Breed muddying your powers. Until you master them all, you will always be at a disadvantage. That's why I'm here. I've been retired from my crossroads duties and have self-appointed myself your private tutor in all things magical and mystical."

"I don't need a private tutor!"

"Oh, but you do! That's why you owe me one! I am doing this out of the kindness of my deceitful heart. Plus, I was hired so you have no choice in the matter."

"Hired! Who? Wait. Adriana."

"You are good at this guessing stuff, aren't you?" Dorie chuckled then polished off the last of her cannoli.

"I'm going to kill her."

"Please! You are all talk. You know darn well you love that insane old lady. You two are so much alike it's like looking into a mirror and seeing the future you."

I hated to admit it to myself, but I knew Pandora was right. I didn't have to like it, however.

"If Adriana trusts you, then I guess I have no choice but to believe in you. But just so you understand, I grew up with Jessica. I will never trust anyone one hundred percent. Being suspicious of anyone and everything is ingrained in me. Jessica jumped at every shadow and with good reason, now that I know what was done to my family. But to get back on track, you said "multiple Breed," just now. I thought only three, witch, shifter, and siren. While unusual, I didn't think it was that odd to have more than one Breed in my lineage."

"Witch, shifter, siren, vampire, and demon. Welcome to the family, Lily. You're a freak show like me!"

If I hadn't been sitting down, I very well may have passed out, or not. Now that I knew what to look for when I was shocked out of my skin. And, oh boy, was I in shock.

LATER THAT EVENING, after watching Dorie put away an entire pound of spaghetti all by herself—including two meatballs, a salad, and a dinner roll—I found myself in my room staring at the ceiling and wondering what tomorrow would bring. Wednesday would be hump day in more ways than one. It meant we had three days left to acquiesce to the demands of the ransom, and/or come up with a plan to find Antonio and destroy the threat of Donna. I started feeling overwhelmed right after dinner and excused myself to wallow in misery alone.

Pandora's revelation that I had the addition of vampire and demon in my bloodline had me reeling. I'd yet to mention any of this to Adelaide or anyone else. The how of it wasn't the issue; the how come no one else *knew* was what had me flummoxed. And what did it mean? Would I suddenly crave human blood and eat the neighbor's cat instead? Would I sprout horns and seek out living on the rim of a volcano to feel hot enough? Were my preconceived notions on what any of this meant real, or was I going to have to relearn what being one heck of a mixed breed paranormal being inferred?

How the hell could Adriana and Antonio, or the Croy side of the family, not be aware of any of this?

What would it mean for me and Lorcan and our tenuous relationship? Would he want to be with someone such as me? Would he want to risk having demon children? I always joked that Adriana was the spawn of everything unholy and evil; I just didn't realize the verity behind that statement! Here I was going around all this time professing that I didn't have an evil fiber in my being, yet I was the progeny of some nefarious imp and a creature that turned into a bat.

Wait, did vampires turn into bats?

See?

Ugh!

What if Dorie was making it all up? I didn't know if I could trust her word.

I heard someone outside my door before the knock sounded. I called out for whomever it was to enter and sat up straitening my clothing while looking over to the door to see who came calling for me. Adelaide stood in the doorway with a slight frown on her face but smiled when she saw the monumental pout I was sporting.

"What is it darling? I told you not to fret over the amount of food you consumed today. Dorie is a champion foodie, and you will have to watch in the future. But I'm positive you will survive the tummy ache that will assuredly materialize sometime tonight."

"It hurts to breathe."

"Oh, darling. You poor dear. Do you want me to call a cleric?"

"No. I deserve this." Groaning, I rolled backward and onto my side, all the while holding my stomach as I pondered the benefits of a well-timed enema.

"Do you want a glass of water?"

"I never want to see food and drink again for as long as I live, which probably won't be through the night at this rate. Ugh."

"I hate to add to your misery, but I came up to tell you I haven't been able to get through to Adriana. I am worried she might have gone off to try and rescue Antonio on her own, or she is plotting something so reprehensible she doesn't want to come in contact with us lest we figure out what diabolical plot she has in store for the prison denizens."

"Do we go find her?" Part of me hoped the answer

would be negative so I could wallow in my misery until my body moved the digestive process along to its final outcome.

"I think we need to. I also think we need to do this alone, don't you? I feel like if we involve the Council, your Uncle Owen, Aunt Chiara, and the rest of your family and friends, we would be at a disadvantage and would have to play by their rules—the Council's. However, if we find Adriana and handle this before anyone realized what we are up to? Do you agree?" Adelaide seemed to hold my opinion in high regard on this matter and it warmed me that my mother thought so highly of it.

I gave it some thought before I responded because I knew what I decided would be what Adelaide would agree to. That was a lot of responsibility and trust, and I wanted to make the right decision.

Before I could say anything on the matter, Pandora knocked and walked in.

"I know what Lily's answer is going to be even before she realizes it herself. However, let me leave you both with this while I go off for a bit this evening. We still need a team—yes, we—I am not about to let you run off and have all the fun without me. While I agree with your mother that we don't need to involve the Council and all their drama, nor get most of your friends and family involved, we still need a team to go in ready for battle."

"Where do we find a team with three days left before the ransom demands need to be addressed?" I asked.

"We have two extremely capable dark witches right in this room. You have luck on your side because I am going to be on your team. I'm heading out tonight to get three more members. That will round us out, and in that time, you need to find and convince Adriana that whatever she has planned can be accomplished with you involved.

Between her and my friends we can sneak into the prison with you two, destroy the army Donna has at her command, and corner that witch before she knows what happened. Not that I think she has an army of any substance at her disposal."

"You don't think she has a multitude of armed minions?"

"I do not. If she did, Donna would be out of there by now, wards or not. She would have sacrificed her front line to bust through any wards and would be out here if that were the case. Do I think she has some kind of small mercenary group keeping her safe and hidden? Yes."

I looked between the two women and again my suspicions arose, causing me to mistrust the intentions of Pandora. I just did not understand why a crossroads demon would align herself with a bunch of witches and invest so much time in our saga.

I could see Dorie acknowledge that the wheels were turning in my mind as I processed all she said with all that I was considering, and she gave me time to ruminate without adding more to the conversation. My mom, Adelaide, was patient as well, anticipating my response, but knowing I needed to chew it over. I groaned inwardly at the food reference I just made, and my stomach responded with a loud, sluggish gurgle of protest.

"Here. Let me help with that." Pandora crossed over to where I was reclined on my bed and touched my stomach. Within seconds I felt a lightening in my midriff and all sense of having been indulgent to the point of exploding, faded.

"How did you do that? *What* did you do for that matter?"

"It's a talent. I was really popular in ancient Egypt. All those feasts and peacock feathers down the throats of the

elite in the vomitorium that the Romans made popular—
so indelicate. One touch by me and those pharaohs gorged
themselves with abandon. Of course, they figured out I
was a demon and tried to entrap me with some kind of
woo-woo magic, but I rewarded that misbehavior with a
hoard of locusts."

Now I *knew* Dorie was pulling my leg because the
ancients purging themselves was a myth, and a long-held
one. I knew from my few years in college that the word
vomitorium was erroneously used as a place where the
wealthy Romans would purge and continue to feast, but in
actuality it was the name they gave the entrance to theaters
or stadiums. A vast difference in what the word came to
mean in modern times. I think she played this game to
hide her true intentions and abilities behind this over-the-
top persona.

Considering I now felt like I hadn't eaten all day, I
wasn't going to call her on her little deceptions and played
along with it. For now.

"I'm in. Just, who do you plan on bringing on board for
this recognizance mission of ours?"

"All in good time, all in good time. Let me run off and
do what needs doing. You and Adelaide get some rest and
tomorrow we can strategize. Plus, you are going to need
time to track down Adriana. I have a feeling she is holed
up in that mansion of hers, elbow-deep in potions and
spells that she intends to let loose on an unsuspecting town.
You need to convince her our plan is the way to go before
she does something we will all regret. Now, I'm off to get
recruits."

That's what worried me. I had no idea what kind of
creatures Pandora considered backup for this mission.
That thought alone would keep me up when I needed all
the rest I could get, that was for certain.

CHAPTER 9

I woke to the sound of bird call the next morning, another sure sign that spring would finally make its long-awaited return. Stretching, I noted the time and was surprised to see not only that I did indeed sleep soundly, but I also slept for two hours longer than I usually do. Pandora had some interesting magic at her disposal, and I wondered how she'd fare in battle. Something told me she'd be virtually invincible, and I suddenly felt a tad more optimistic than I did yesterday.

I swung my legs off the bed and stepped down to wriggle my feet into my waiting slippers only to pull my legs up quickly as Wicked shot out from under me hissing and spitting.

"Well, you shouldn't have been lying on the floor on top of my slippers you nutcase!"

Heading to the shower, I paused long enough to peer out the window, making note of the weather. The sky was clear and there was a slight breeze. I wondered if the warming trend would continue or if we had more bad weather heading our way. Checking my phone, I verified we would remain in the fifties, so I grabbed the other set of the super ninja clothing my mom made for me. Before I was completed with my morning ritual, my thoughts went to Pandora and her mystery backups. I wondered again about who, or what, she would show up with today.

Heading downstairs, I found Wicked getting love and sympathy from my mom. I barely touched her, yet she was acting like I crushed her under my feet!

Adelaide had coffee made and was dressed in a similar manner to my outfit of choice. A plate of biscotti was on the table and she had the radio on low with '80s tunes playing. The Pet Shop Boys were dolling the virtues of making lots of money.

"Morning. Have you heard from Granny? Or Pandora for that matter?"

"Good morning, darling. Pandora, no, but I managed to reach Adriana just before turning in for the night. She agreed to meeting with us and is catching a ride with Lorcan. I believe he has finished her car and will run it over to her, and she will bring him back to town."

Lorcan! In all this brouhaha, I'd forgotten to have that talk with him. It still rankled that he'd been so enamored of the lovely new deputy, but now that I had time to cool down and think straight, I could see how Tiffany was purposely trying to get under my skin and make more of her and Lorcan's past. It still didn't explain why he'd never mentioned the woman. Especially since I'd asked him point blank if any other old flames would turn up out of the woodwork, and he'd denied any more existed.

Men! Sometimes I think they were put on earth for the sole purpose to age women faster than we would without their BS. That and for spider removal. And yard work. Ugh.

Maybe I could carve a few moments for the two of us

now, when Adriana dropped him off in a few. I had to make time to head over to my studio since I had a few packages to ship out. In all the bad weather we experienced over the last three weeks, I'd had plenty of time to work on projects, but now I needed to mail them to the people who had consigned them and see if any new orders came in. I couldn't wait for the new fairground to open and the crafting booths that promised even more income for me.

My sculpting studio had taken off and I was getting low on supplies, so that too would be a project I'd have to add to my long list of things to do in the next few weeks. I only hoped the drama would be a distant memory in a few days and we'd be well on our way to removing the threat of Donna and returning my dad once we got the answers we needed from her.

That's another reason why I wanted to make peace with Lorcan. Life was way too short, even for witchfolk. When I thought of what my parents lost and all their years apart, I didn't want to let petty issues be a distraction, or lead to acrimony when it came to our relationship.

Just then, I heard the telltale sound of tires on gravel and knew I'd get that chance sooner rather than later.

"Morning, Squirt. You ready to fight the good fight?" Adriana came bustling in my back door all business, but she couldn't fool me. Her face was drawn and her eyes sunken and lifeless shadowed by the dark circles under them. I knew she must have been up for days worrying about Antonio. I also knew she was beyond angry with the Council and must be feeling some level of betrayal by their apathy. I know I did. It bolstered the nagging feeling I had that influences outside our family were stirring up trouble and causing a rift in the Council—those that supported my family and those that wanted to usurp us and step into a power position.

"Good morning, Grandmother. I *am* ready to fight, good or otherwise. Let's sit and enjoy some coffee and plan this out. Mom is on her way down and Pandora should be around here somewhere. I just need to make a quick trip over to my studio to take care of a few things, then I'm all yours."

Adelaide walked in just as I finished explaining my need to delay our meeting and went straight for Adriana and enveloped her in a massive hug. "I promise I will be right back. It won't take me but a minute or two—or ten!"

"Go. We will have our coffee and a light breakfast. Pandora will be back soon; she just called me."

Ok, then. I didn't know our friendly demon used a cell phone. Or maybe she called from the lone surviving pay phone on the outskirts of town. Who knew?

I dashed out the door and over to my Jeep. Sitting in the driver's seat was Wicked, looking smug and ready for a zip around the square. I didn't have time to scold her, let alone wait for her to hop out, so I threw open the door and said, "Move!"

I received a scathing look, but Wicked did hop onto the passenger side and proceeded to look out her window. Shaking my head at my cat's seemingly endless talents— opening a locked Jeep right up there as the most compelling—I turned on the engine and pulled onto my street.

As I approached the square, I could see the local businesses were already busy with foot traffic and the occasional local shoppers making the rounds. I noticed Hester and Chester Soule outside their funeral parlor in front of the glossy black hearse they used for transport and ceremonies. A worker in a plain grey uniform was wheeling a coffin out of the back and I couldn't seem to pull my eyes away from the scene. Especially since the greenish, glowing aura of the ghost of Orville Crawley was hovering just outside the vehicle, wringing his hands and looking all manner of lost.

Just then, he whipped his head in my direction, eyes going wide.

Oh, no. No, no, no! Not again! I knew he saw me and recognized that I could see him in return. What kind of ghost magnet was I? How on earth could he know I was driving by and realize I could see him in his ghostly form? I made to gun my engine and speed away lest he try to nab me, but just then, Wicked reached her paw out and gave me a soft, "Mreow?"

Unbelievably, I understood what she was telling me. Better I go interview the ghost and see what Orville knew and perhaps get the password, key, or whatever spell was needed to enter the prison then miss the opportunity for any insight he may give, just because I didn't want another ghost hanging around—and moving in with me.

"Ugh!" I hated this with every fiber of my being. Instead of continuing on to my studio, I turned and pulled to the curb in front of the funeral home just in front of the hearse, then parked. Chester saw me exit my Jeep and beamed at me which was disconcerting considering he didn't seem to have a bottom lip in sight. He was all wiry mustache and overbite and it made him look like a demented puppet, sans string. Hester was barking orders at the hapless employee who kept shaking his head and waving his arms at the hearse.

"What's up, Chester. Is something wrong?" I looked everywhere and didn't see the ghost of Orville Crawley any longer, which I found odd. I thought for sure it was me he was excited to see and would have stuck around long enough for an interview, or the proverbial shoulder to cry on, since I could see and hear his tale of woe. But he was nowhere in sight.

"Sister is upset because we've had a tree come down during the ice storm and it has blocked the drive leading around the back of our business. She thinks it unseemly for the general public to have to see one of our customers be wheeled in the front door."

I could see why she felt the need for discretion. Hermione and Hortense Winters were staring daggers at the brother and sister duo from behind the windows of their tea shop, and I assumed any customers enjoying tea and sympathy or buying any of the many wares the two sisters sold at their place of business was find it off-putting to look up and see a coffin drift by. Even if we were a town of witches, many of us had the heebie-jeebies around the Soules and their chosen profession.

"Um, did you happen to notice anything unusual while unloading the, er, deceased just now?" I asked.

"Why, now that you mention it, poor Orville Crawley was whirling about looking all distressed and out of sorts. I was going to inform you of this when we caught up with you later today, but here you are now, so I guess you could try and communicate with him. Now, where did he get to, I wonder? He was shouting something odd about traitorous tears, or teas, or was that trajectile teens? No matter, we will figure it out."

"No time for that! No time for that! We need to get his corpse attended to. His spirit is out of our hands," Hester cried, her short, round frame wriggling with indignation and exasperation. She was as short and stout as Chester was tall, lanky, and downright skeletal.

"Hello, Lily. We are too busy for social niceties right

now, dear. Run along and we will see you once we get our body settled into a nice cooler in the basement."

Ick.

Wait a minute.

"What do you mean, you will see me later? I didn't know I'd be seeing you today at all, and..."

"Don't bump the coffin trolley into the railing! Are you blind? You fool! Chester, get over here and help this imbecile into the building before he manages to knock the coffin off the transport. My word, help these days!"

Chester gave me an apologetic shrug and loped over to help get Orville Crawley's remains into the building. Where the man's spirit wound up would be a mystery, not unlike that little comment from Hester Soule. Maybe she misspoke or the siblings were under the impression we had a meeting of some sort.

I didn't have time to worry about any of this since I was now late getting to my studio and time was ticking.

Throwing a farewell wave to the Winters sisters, I hopped back into my Jeep and made a U-turn, then parked outside of my studio where I got out only to find Lorcan waiting. He was leaning up against George, my old blue truck used for my arrival in Sweet Briar several months back. While George still ran and could be counted on in the fall and winter, his AC was busted and he didn't have tinted windows which would be hell come spring and summer, so I had used some of my inheritance to buy my new Jeep, Gypsy. Yes, I name my vehicles. Doesn't everyone?

"Hey." Hopping down from my seat, I held the door open for Wicked who ran out and began weaving in and around Lorcan's ankles.

"Hey."

We stood staring at one another for a good minute, then Lorcan broke the awkward silence.

"I missed your face."

"I don't like fighting. I also don't like lies."

Sighing, Lorcan looked down at Wicked then back at me.

"Do you have time to talk?"

"Not really I'm already running late. I should have been back at the house already; my mother and Adriana are waiting for me. I am here to grab packages that need to be shipped and then running back. I got sidetracked by the Soules, sort of."

"I could handle the shipping for you. Lily, wait." Lorcan held up his hand as I was about to protest then ran it through his rich brown hair in frustration. "I didn't say anything about Tiffany because I haven't thought about her in years. Not only that, but she never was a thing! Not to me anyway!"

Glancing around, I noticed Maureen watching from June's Emporium, not to mention the deputy herself who occupied a window booth at Joe's Diner with our sheriff. I guess they were having breakfast. She raised her coffee cup giving me a little salute and I wanted to hit her with a Tormentum Mortis spell right between those baby blues. Or not. I wasn't that dark.

Yet.

"Can we go inside and continue? I feel exposed out here. It's like the entire town knows our business before we do."

Lorcan waited for me to unlock the garage door that opened into the alley between our two shops, and followed me in, Wicked on his heels.

"It's the Gossip Gang. I swear, nothing is sacred in this town. I found out I was contemplating suicide from Becky, who heard it from Doreen Murphy, who swore she heard my mother lamenting at the doctor's office just yesterday. It's a wonder I didn't wake up to find both of my parents standing over me gnashing their teeth with worry from all the rumors."

"If Tiffany meant nothing to you, what's with her story about you and Nora and her role in breaking you up? And the husband crack. What was that about?" I crossed my arms and waited to hear what he had to say for himself and the bizarre insinuations Tiffany had made.

"That! We went through a phase in high school where all the kids who were dating began calling their boyfriends and girlfriends "husband and wife." I dated Tiffany for a week, I think. I mean, we were friends. We dated and kissed a few times then one day she was dating Gregory Miller and I moved on to the cute sophomore whose name I seriously cannot remember because the following week I decided to swear off girls until college."

"She didn't break you and Nora up?"

"Only in the sense that when Nora was being her horrible self, I mentioned that she could use lessons on how to be nice from someone like Tiffany. Tiffany never made anyone feel bad or picked on. She was popular *and* nice. Nora was one of those mean girls. But not Tiff." Lorcan declared.

I rolled my eyes in disgust at his addled perception.

"Oh, you poor, delusional man, you," I snarked. "Lorcan, you are a good guy. A nice guy. Seriously, you might be *too* nice. And because of this you refuse to see bad in anyone. Tiffany is not nice. Not to me anyway. Not to any female she deems a threat or in the way of something she desires. And if I had to guess, I'd say it is you, right now, who she desires."

"If you say so. I don't see it, Lily. I'm not saying you're

87

wrong. I believe you. But the girl I knew would not act like that."

I sighed inwardly and gave it one more shot. "People change, Lorcan. All the time. Just keep that in mind, will you?"

"So, we're OK?" Lorcan looked so hopeful and woebegone that I couldn't stay mad with him, especially knowing he didn't purposefully hide a relationship with Tiffany from me. I could see how to him they had a friendship, but for what she intended, they were an item.

"We're OK."

Lorcan opened his arms, and I went to him. We spent a few precious moments in a mildly heated embrace, a respite from the rest of the world. But then I was reminded by Wicked that we needed to return home despite my wanting a few more minutes wrapped up in Lorcan and my happy place. She actually bit my ankle to get my attention. She got it.

"Ow! You evil snot. That hurt."

"Here, let me take these packages for you and send them out. You run home and take care of whatever Adriana has cooked up, but please be careful. I'm not going to go all he-man on you and demand you stay out of the thick of things. I know you need to do this. Just promise that you will keep me posted on what's up and be careful? Please?"

"I promise. I will call or text when I get a handle on this situation and what I intend to do about it."

I reached up to give Lorcan another kiss and turned to leave when he stopped me.

"Hey, Lily?"

I turned back with questioning eyes and Lorcan continued.

"I love you."

Smiling and melting a bit at this kind man who happened to be a big, dumb, dope when it came to vindictive women, I blew him a kiss and responded with my own, "I love you too."

I rushed back to my Jeep and made it home in record time. And unfamiliar car was parked on my gravel driveway and I puzzled at who could be visiting, thinking maybe it was whomever Pandora stated she'd be bringing into our battle. When I walked in my home, that theory was confirmed when I saw who was sitting at my kitchen table.

"Mortimer! And Caliente! It's so nice to see you again! Are you who Pandora thought to bring with us to take care of Donna?"

"Indeed, but not just the two of us. You see, Pandora has suggested two more people skilled in the type of mission we are about go on."

Puzzled I looked at Pandora who was snickering with glee then followed the flick of her wrist as she pointed to two more people I'd not noticed before.

"Hello."

Chester Soule! And Hester tittering behind him!

Was Pandora out of her mind? Looking back over to the demon who was now openly laughing and making googly eyes at me, I'd have to say the answer was an emphatic *yes!*

CHAPTER 10

"Tell me again why we are bringing those two?" I asked as I drove Adriana, who was riding shotgun, and my mother, who was in the back seat with Pandora. I was following Mortimer, my friendly vampire friend and his girlfriend, Caliente, also a vampire. They had the Soules with them, and I still could not for the life of me understand why.

"The Soules have a skill set which makes them invaluable," Pandora explained.

"The Soules. Chester and Hester. Him so tall he'd knock his head off running through the caverns in the prison, and she of the rotund variety so much so, she'd more than likely get stuck in a tight passage. Those two?"

"Don't fat-shame poor Hester. She can't help that she's so short her body became that wide!" Adriana sniffed.

"I'm not fat-shaming, I am fact-stating the obvious! She gets stuck in the doorways of her own place of business and complained just last week that the booths at Joe's were too small after she got stuck trying to sit down in one. I'm not being mean! Hester is short and wide!" I protested.

"She knows she's wide. She's usually proud of her girth until she gets stuck somewhere, hence my point!" I would never be so mean as to judge someone by the way they look, but we were on a stealth mission that would lead to some kind of battle. I couldn't see those two being any kind of asset and felt someone needed to point out the evidence staring plainly at us!

Pandora laughed with delight at my continued doubt regarding the siblings and their prowess in the upcoming battle.

"And Chester. Don't pretend you didn't notice the small piece of flesh he had Hester sew back on his forehead! He rammed his noggin on the corner shelf at Becky's bookstore. Books flew in every direction and he tripped over his own feet trying to gather them back up. He is constantly smacking into things and then apologizes even if it's an inanimate object," I protested.

Everyone just smiled at me, so I knew they were humoring me and my foul mood.

"Look, Chester spent ten minutes telling a coatrack he didn't see it last week at June's Emporium! And another thing. He constantly makes that odd slurping sound, not to mention he clears his throat every flipping minute like clockwork. Donna will hear him coming a mile before he reaches her! I still have no idea what this 'skill set' of theirs entails!" I groused.

"They are illusionists of the highest order. We need a distraction to have time to build up the kind of magic we will need to take Donna and her minions out. They key to this battle is not the number of soldiers we bring to fight, it's how much time the few that *will* be fighting have to make the most of the magic expelled. Our desire is to hit the mark the first time. To do that we need a distraction so we can let our magic coil up and reach the levels which will render Donna useless yet still keep her alive, while destroying everything else in her wake," Pandora chided me.

"But... but, I don't think I quite understand," I lamented, hating that I still didn't know everything there was to know about magic.

"Lily, darling. It takes a certain amount of power to finesse the outcome we desire. We don't want to go into the prison guns blazing, so to speak. We need Donna alive and well, contained, but uninjured if we are to get answers to the questions we seek. She is our only hope to be able to understand where your father is and what type of magic was used on his mind to keep him away from us for so long. If he's alive, something has kept him away, after all." Adelaide explained.

"I just can't believe our mission's success is dependent on those two. I mean, Chester smells like a cheeseburger. Why does Chester always smell of cheeseburger? Why? Can anyone here give me a succinct explanation of how the man manages to have that odor prevalent when he doesn't appear to have had that particular meal in ages? I don't mean a mild whiff, like he might have had a burger for lunch. I mean, full blown, burger on the grill, with melting cheese on a bun with pickles and ketchup kind of in your face aroma! It's inexplicable!"

"She has a point, you know." This from Adriana who always seemed to take my side in the oddest of times.

"I hardly think Chester's body odor is cause for concern. Not when he can do such incredible illusions only a virtuoso, a master proficient in the same, would be able to see past." Pandora stated.

I kept blinking in frustrated confusion. My mind just could not wrap itself around such revelations. "Even Hester? She is that skilled?"

"Hester can perform illusions almost as well as her brother. But that is *not* why I asked her to join our team," Pandora explained. "Hester can deceive and influence outcomes by impelling a weaker mind to do her bidding. And almost everyone I know has a mind weaker than hers."

What? I did not think I had a weak mind. What about Adelaide? And Adriana? Did everyone on this mission really believe Hester was the superior when it came to mind games? That the rest of us should kowtow to her because of perceived exceptional abilities?

"What can she do?" I asked in wonder.

"Hester can read minds before the person she is reading even knows what they are themselves thinking, or about to say. She can read a person better than anyone I know. But that's not all, she can create an illusion inside someone's mind. They are so strong, the person being influenced cannot tell reality from falsehood that is happening on the inside, in their own thoughts. Can you imagine how useful this will be for us on this particular enterprise? Hester can make Donna believe she has already won the battle leaving her vulnerable to our attack," Pandora proclaimed.

Well, then.

Mortimer and Caliente were assets because they were both vampires. Plus, both could virtually figure out how to dismantle any magical barrier blocking our way given enough time—so why they were chosen made sense. I just had to go with the other opinions regarding the Soules' involvement.

How did we find out the new location for the prison? Did Gloria come through with it for us?" I asked no one in particular.

Adriana answered with a grimace. "Gloria was

forbidden from telling any of us where it is. The Council have watchers making sure she doesn't try to contact us. I believe they have a listening device on her phone if you can imagine that! I swear, once this is over and done, I am going to turn that Council upside down and find out who is thwarting our family, and making life difficult. And after everything the Dolce clan has done for this town and our many contributions to the Council itself. I mean really!"

I could understand my great-grandmother's frustration and disappointment. It was a betrayal whose scars ran deep. I thought the Dietrich and Langsford clans were acting alone, but not with this kind of blockade and red tape constantly obstructing our family's wants and needs.

If anyone would get to the bottom of it, it would be Adriana. I intended to be right there by her side when she did.

"Who is going to cause the distraction to keep the Council busy and out of our hair? I thought just me and possibly one other person would slip in, but now I have a posse!"

"We decided on Abner. He's been going around the town setting off a slew of *hijinks* curses which are unpredictable but harmless. The Council must be getting complaint after complaint about now, and I know he's planning a direct attack in their chambers. They are holding a meeting today to decide what to do about you, Lily. Serves them right for even considering you might need disciplinary action even though Tiffany chose not to pursue charges."

How nice of her. Like I trusted it was a show of goodwill on her part. Not.

"So, how do we know where we are going?" I wondered.

"Hester spoke with Orville. He was the only other

person alive—or in his case, dead—that knew of the next location scheduled. The Council votes on where the doorway will appear each time, then it is passed on to Gloria, who in turn gives it to the warden. Orville was last week's warden and unless they've changed it since he's been murdered, its location should be the same place they decided on for this week." Adelaide said.

"And that is where, exactly?"

"Turn right here, Squirt. We've arrived at its location," Adriana informed me.

I almost stopped short which would have caused one heck of a fender bender. Instead, I slowed as I signaled and turned into the parking lot of a place I'd least expect the new entrance of the witch prison would be.

"The Everlasting Love of The Lord Upon High Holy Redeemer Evangelical Church is the secret entrance to the witch prison? Really?" I couldn't believe Oliver and Laura Brewster's humble place of worship was what the Council decided on. I mean, how did they even decide such things and who's bright idea was to stick it in an evangelical church?

"The basement is, anyway," Adriana cackled. "Let's go see if we can sneak in before the Brewsters even know what hit them."

Surely this would not go down according to plan. How could it?

§

"WHAT DID YOU EXPECT? I mean really! What did you think would happen when the lot of us waltzed into a church in the late morning on a weekday dragging two vampires and a guy who looks like Ichabod Crane's taller brother, followed by a midget witch festooned in a rather garishly pointy witch hat?"

It went down exactly as I expected it would. Well, maybe not entirely the way I expected. After all, I didn't know Laura Brewster would throw such a monumental hissy fit sending the choir after us with hymn books flapping. Nor did I think being hit by the tiny hymnals would hurt as much as it did.

Nor did I think Minerva and Hettie, two of the choir ladies in the congregation, would have such strong sets of teeth seeing as how both of the women were nearing their nineties if they hadn't already reached such a lofty age. My leg still smarted where Hettie clamped down, while my arm still bore the marks of Minerva's rather vice-like grip. It took me ten minutes to pry open her dentures and remove them from where they were hanging from my weenus, er, the excessive soft skin when my elbow is not bent, that is.

The rest of the choir had attacked my group with gleeful abandon while singing the praises of the Lord. Beulah, she of the deep voice and scripture pontificating from the last time we met, had even brandished a broom, swinging it at Mortimer's head like a baseball bat. He'd be pulling plastic bristles out of his skin for the next week, so efficient was Beulah at nailing him on his noggin.

Right now, we were trying to figure out what to do about the lot of them, tied up and sitting on the floor of the church while we blockaded the entry in case any more from their congregation decided to show up.

"Oh, look, Minerva! It's the Papist. Remember her, dear? Only her intelligent friend isn't with her this time. And she's dressed like one of those Satanist tarts you see in the movies, like that Angelina Jolie person." Hettie declared, giving me the once-over.

Hey! Wait a minute. If Andrea was the intelligent one, what did they consider me?

"And a New Yorker! I told you one can never trust a Yankee," Minerva nodded in agreement and bequeathed me the old stink eye.

Oh, well that explains it.

"What are you doing? Take your hands off me! Take your filthy hands off me!" Laura Brewster was screeching at the top of her lungs and acting like we were pummeling her into submission when all Caliente did was escort her to a pew.

"Lady, if you don't shut it, I will give you something to really scream about," Pandora wasn't amused by the overzealous attack on her person nor the sniveling Laura who'd summed up our gang in one succinct observation.

"Demons! The lot of you!" Laura cried.

"Now, Laura, honey. Don't rile up these folks until we know what they want with us." Oliver, ever the pragmatist, chided his spouse while giving Pandora the once-over. The gleam in his eye and approval at what he beheld made me suspect he'd switch to her side if he thought he'd have a modicum of a chance at realizing whatever foul thoughts he was having about her. My skin was crawling yet again over the vile preacher. Why he couldn't be more like Father Reedy at my mother's old church was beyond me. That man was a poster boy for everything good and holy, and it always amazed me at how outnumbered a man such as he was in our world.

While Oliver was transfixed by the visage that was Pandora, he was positively overcome when he noticed my mother in the group.

"Adelaide! Is that you? Why, I never thought I'd ever see you again, my dear. How lovely," he gushed.

"Lovely! Lovely? She is a degenerate. An evil, vile,

wanton creature. I forbid you to even speak to her another minute!" Laura cried. She was even frothing at the mouth a little.

Oliver blanched and gave my mother an apologetic look while he tried to appease his wife at the same time. I don't think it worked.

Adelaide rolled her eyes and gave Oliver a withering glance. She didn't even bother saying one word, then turned to me raising both eyebrows while mimicking a gag reflex. I giggled which only started Laura up again.

"They want to perform vile acts upon us! May the good Lord smite them where they stand!" Laura howled, spittle flying in all directions.

We all looked up at the ceiling at exactly the same time, and when nothing happened—no lightning bolts, or thumb of God coming down to flatten us—I for one, turned my frown into a smirk which I made sure Laura could see.

What surprised me was the look of sadness on Pandora's face. I thought she'd be having a blast torturing these souls. Instead, she seemed almost pensive and saddened at their behavior. She caught me looking and shrugged. "They make my job easy. I almost wish it wasn't the case. They are supposed to be the good guys—and some truly are—but people like these folks? Not so much." She sighed and we got down to business.

"Where is it then? The entrance?" I asked.

"In the basement," Hester replied, looking grim. Her hat got damaged in the scuffle and she was feeling rather pouty. I couldn't really blame her. It was a nice hat before the choir tore it to shreds. "You head down there now while I make this lot forget everything they've seen and heard. I will knock them out with a sleep spell then we can release them when we return from our little objective. Shall we?"

We all trudged down the steps to the lower level of the church and the first thing I noticed was the odor of mold and mustiness. The second thing I noticed was an old cabinet that had an unearthly glow coming from its depths.

"I do believe I have found our entrance," I proclaimed. That's when all the lights went out and I felt a sharp stab hit my left temple.

CHAPTER 11

"**H**ow are we supposed to fight off a hoard of evil minions if we forgot to case the joint for other church members? Ow! That old bat must have a claw hammer in her purse," I complained, rubbing my head which I'm sure already sported a bruise.

I looked over at the offending assailant. Yet another choir member, I presumed. This one even more birdlike than Hettie and Minerva, also sporting a head of blue-tinted grey hair, clutching her purse even though Mortimer held her arms tight lest she take another swing at us.

"Ball-peen."

"What?"

"I have a ball-peen hammer in my purse."

Well, that explains my momentary loss of consciousness. At least this time I hadn't blacked out from some stupid coagulation of my witch magic meeting siren magic causing me to get my circuits crossed!

"Don't you realize you can kill someone if you hit them with that thing?" I asked.

"Of course, dear. That's why I carry it."

Lovely. We have a homicidal, octogenarian church lady on our hands.

"Are you going to rough me up now?"

"Do you want us to, um, what's your name, anyway?"

"Juliette. Juliette Chrysanthemum Howard. I would like fair warning so I can prepare to meet my maker should you choose to rough me up. I don't think I will survive, I'm eighty-two, you see."

"This one is slightly over one hundred," I pointed to Adriana then continued, "and she managed to tackle you to the ground. I doubt you'd have any trouble withstanding anything we plan on doing to you, Juliette."

Juliette looked positively crestfallen with the news.

"Oh! I so did want to try out my Krav Maga moves. Perhaps next time." Juliette simpered.

Krav...what?

"We don't have time for this, people! Tie her up and bring her to Hester. She can work her memory magic and then join us so we can get on with it already!" Adriana barked.

"I'll pray for your souls." Juliette proclaimed as Mortimer shuffled her up the steps to Hester.

I left the group to head back to the iron door that was surely the entrance to the witch prison. Someone at the Council had a dark sense of humor to place it in the basement of the Evangelical church, and I wanted to smack them. There had to be some way to open the door, and I hoped Hester or Chester knew what it was, since they spoke with Orville Crawley.

Adelaide joined me and together we felt all around for some kind of latch or knob or other mechanism that would get us on the other side. I didn't detect any wards other than the glow and wondered what that could mean.

"Do you think it's spelled?" I asked my mother.

Adelaide stepped back and looked at the door with her chin in her hand. Then she tilted her head to one side and squinted at the hinges.

"What if we remove these pins? Wouldn't we be able to lift the door and get in by doing that?"

"Ahem. If I may." Chester squeezed between me and Adelaide and bent in half, his nose mere inches from the iron door. The odor of cheeseburger slammed into me and I gave my mother a pointed look as he continued his observations. "There is a keyhole. Orville said we would receive the magic key once someone learned the password."

"Please tell me you know the password," I practically pleaded.

"No. But Hester said we would be met by someone who did."

What? Another surprise member of the team? Who would show up now? Stu Jones? Gordy Polk? Joe?

Just as Hester made it down the steps to join us in the basement, I felt something brush against my ankles and let out a loud shriek. Looking down, I saw Wicked at my feet, a key tied around her neck.

"Seriously? Wicked knows the password?"

"Orville refused to tell us, not wanting to break his oath of office or some such, even in death. So, he whispered it to Wicked and here she is to save the day!" Hester replied as she came to stand beside her brother.

I still doubted the odd duo would be an asset to the team, and thought we had a better chance of success if we took anyone else along for the ride. Even Hermione and Hortense and their oversexed, enthusiastic spellcasting would be better than these two. I had just finished the thought then winced, waiting for Hester or Chester to scold me, so often had they read my mind in the past. When I saw the two blink in surprise and glance at each other, I realized the lessons I had been doing with Adelaide had paid off tenfold. The Soules could no longer read my thoughts!

I gave them a snug smile with a jaunty salute then reached down to remove the key from Wicked's collar.

"Do we have any idea who the new warden is? And will we meet them on the other side of this doorway?" I asked.

"We should. It's a running prison and we are going in the main entrance. Even though they've discouraged visitors, some still have family incarcerated or have their attorneys visit. You know, we should have brought Jake with us. We might have been able to have him sweet-talk us inside, instead of doing what we are about to do," Adriana mused.

The door swung open and we entered a large reception area bustling with prison workers, all who looked up in shock as we advanced.

"What are we about to do?" I whispered in sotto voice.

"This!"

Bam!

Adriana sent a streak of purple sparks across the room at the same time Hester threw an orange smoky powder flying which enveloped the workers, rendering them immobile. Their eyes went vacant and they slumped to the floor en masse, but just before they hit the ground, Adriana's magic settled them gently, so they didn't suffer any injuries.

"That went rather well," Adriana cackled, then stormed through the reception room heading for a pair of double doors on the far side opposite our entrance.

We were finally going to get some answers. This was going to be epic!

CHAPTER 12

This was so far from epic that I don't think a word existed that could explain it. We were walking. We'd been walking now going on thirty minutes and there was no end in sight to the winding corridors and endless staircases. I refused to complain because I didn't want to be cast as the whining kvetch that held up the rest of the team and made everyone's life miserable. But this sucked. Like, big time.

I kept a maniacal-looking grin on my face that even I knew wasn't fooling anyone, but I refused to mention the obvious. This was taking way too long, and my feet were getting tired and achy. I assume everyone else felt the same, but again, I wasn't going to be the first to say anything.

I was incredulous that Hester had managed to keep up, especially with the loping stride of Mortimer and the gracefully long legs of Caliente. They were making me irate, because at five foot three, I had to put a giddy-up to my step to stay alongside their strides. My disposition was soured even more since Adriana led the way—her coat flapping behind as she went hither and yon, seeming to know the direction we were to take. Wicked was perched on her shoulder and they made the odd image as we continued heading lower and lower into the penitentiary.

We hadn't come upon any more prison workers but occasionally I could hear sounds coming from behind the locked doors that we strode by. They looked just like the doors one saw in the movies or on television that usually denoted solitary confinement. I wondered who the hapless prisoners were that resided behind each ingress.

Another doorway led to another corridor, and beyond that another flight of steps heading downward. This kept repeating until I thought I'd go insane with the monotony of it all. I thought the three-mile walk Adriana and I had done to access the lower levels of the Forbidden Library was awful. This was pure torture, however!

I was pulled out of my morose reverie when I sensed a change in atmosphere. The very air around us became stifled and heavy, and a vibration echoed off the very walls that seemed to close in around us.

"Do you hear that sound?" I murmured.

"For the last five minutes," Caliente responded quietly.

Mortimer nodded and I understood it to mean that he, too, had heard it for longer than the rest of my crew. It made me wonder why the rest of us hadn't noticed unless vampires had super-hearing or some such. That no longer mattered since we collectively paused upon hearing another, more disturbing sound coming from just up ahead. It was a slurping, sniveling wheeze that seemed to come from multiple sources and I knew at once what I was hearing.

"Sentinels!" I uttered hoarsely, as the hairs on my body rose.

"Well, now we know where they've been all this time. Guarding the blockade keeping Donna and her army in and anyone from this side of the prison out," Adriana murmured sullenly.

"Now what do we do?" Adelaide wondered aloud.

"We have to find a way around them, that is all," Mortimer stated.

"Or through them," Caliente finished.

"Please. We have to eliminate them, or they will follow us incessantly. If this is the only way in or out of the lower level now that the old secret entrance Morty here guarded has been permanently sealed, it's no wonder Donna has been stuck and not able to make her escape. Not even she can get by these beasts. They make the ones in the Forbidden Library look like kindergarteners in comparison," Pandora proclaimed, not bothering to lower her voice. The Sentinels began to grumble and moan, so I knew they could hear her.

Thankfully, they must be on the other side of whatever blockade was in place or they would have been upon us by now. This was verified when we turned the final corner and were confronted by a huge arch with a whirling vortex of shimmering magic as the barrier we suspected we'd find.

"Oh, this looks like loads of fun!" Pandora cried.

The Sentinels could just be made out on the other side and they surged forward as the sound of her voice reached them.

"Well, there goes any hope of Donna not realizing someone is at her front door, so to speak," I bemoaned throwing a scowl Pandora's way.

"Oops!" She giggled and gave me an eyebrow wag. "My bad!"

I was about to continue my scolding, but an unholy roar sounded all around us and I had visions of goblins streaming out of cracks and crevices like in *Lord of the Rings*.

I was certain they were about to descend upon us and rip us to shreds.

"Now what? What is making that noise?"

"Um, perhaps they are to blame?" Mortimer thrust his chin up and when we tracked our eyes up in the direction he pointed. I noticed what first appeared to be a tall ceiling above us was actually a seemingly endless circular space with open arches going upward without an end in sight. Peering out of the arches were bluish-grey creatures that looked slick and warty at the same time. The smell hit me before I knew what was happening and I gagged. It smelled like roadkill and I didn't think I'd ever be able to ride around with the top off of my Jeep after this.

"What are those things? Baby Sentinels? They are oozing!"

"Those are trolls," Adriana stated.

"Trolls! Trolls? I thought trolls were huge, and dumb, and *huge*! These things are freakishly skinny, oozing pustules of goop! What the... gah!" As they leaned over to get a better look at us, or so I assumed, they began to drip. Like snotty goo drip. And I felt like one of those kids who gets slimed on Nickelodeon.

I began to whimper and edged closer to my mother.

Hester pulled an umbrella out of her skirt and opened it. Who carries an umbrella around with them? It didn't stop me from changing my trajectory and sidling up to her instead of Adelaide.

"Ahem. Does anyone else feel hot?" Chester asked and began fiddling with his collar.

Pandora looked round and shrugged. "I don't know. It kinda feels nice to me."

Well, it would, wouldn't it?

"Maybe that's because the walls are glowing red hot,"

Adriana pointed out, making us all huddle closer to the center of the corridor.

"This makes no sense. How could the Council or prison guards not know about this? The barrier should not have any such occurrences on this side. If we were on the side where Donna Fredricks is housed, then I could understand this," Caliente complained. "This is impossible. How could we have stumbled into a trap even before reaching the other side?"

Pandora had wandered over to one of the walls and sniffed. "Smells like sulfur. Fire and brimstone and all that jazz. Heh, feels like home." She touched her finger to the surface, and it began to sizzle which made me jump. Pandora licked her fingertip and the crackling stopped. Sniffing her finger, she chuckled. "It smells like a toasted marshmallow."

"We need to head back the way we came in a hurry before anything else happens. Then we can reconvene at a later date when we've sought information from the Council. Obviously, something is amiss," Caliente suggested.

I didn't particularly want to retreat, but I couldn't figure out what to do about the trolls and the super-heated walls. Perhaps Caliente has the right idea and we could try again tomorrow, although I knew we were running out of time. Just as we turned to backtrack the way we had come, the floor under our feet tilted and we slid in haphazardly toward the barrier.

This was going to hurt.

I braced myself for what I assumed would be one magical ass-whupping, only to find myself unhurt and much cooler in a chamber on the opposite side of the barricade. Not a Sentinel in sight, nor a hoard of monsters. Instead, the air was clean, free of the smell of trolls, and if anything, scented with what was unmistakably that of vanilla.

"What happened? Was that an illusion?" I turned to Hester and Chester who had their heads together whispering furiously and nodding. Hey, they were supposed to be illusion experts. I assumed they would know.

"Hmmm, ahem, yes! I do believe we have just been fooled by very heavy wards put up by the Council, which means we are probably still not at the point of entry for the lower prison level. Perhaps we should walk on a bit and see where this hallway leads," Chester suggested.

I wanted to slap him silly. The last thing I wanted to do was continue walking.

"Great idea. Let's walk."

What? I wasn't going to be the sourpuss of the group. If they could walk, so could I. Blisters be damned.

❧

"I DIDN'T EXPECT THIS. Well, I expected another barrier of sorts but not this." I stated as we came to an iron gate with sharp, pointy toppers that looked impenetrable. We had walked for another thirty minutes, I kid you not, and I would have gladly thrown myself on the spikes if it meant not having to go another foot.

"Now this looks more like something the Council would erect to impede any forward progress to the lower levels. That arch back there was over-the-top drama. Illusions to make a lesser immortal run in fear," Mortimer sniffed.

I might not be immortal, but I would have gladly run if those troll things continued to rain down their snot in an unending mass of goo. I knew an hour-long shower awaited me once I returned home from this fun little outing. Hester shook off her umbrella and put it away, but the sounds of goop hitting the floor as she did so would give me nightmares for weeks. I knew I'd always look up before going to be forevermore, hoping I'd see a nice smooth ceiling above me but fearing it would suddenly open up to reveal that horror I just experienced.

I heard a crackling sound behind me and turned in time to see Chester stuff what looked suspiciously like a Kit Kat into his mouth.

"You brought snacks?" I asked hopefully.

Chester swallowed loudly then looked sheepish. "My blood sugar plummets if I don't have a bit of something. I'd offer to share, but it's too late, as I don't have another."

I told him not to sweat it, seeming magnanimous, although in reality I wanted to rip his head off. I was starved and knew I was being petulant and childish, but I really could have used some chocolate. The telltale sign that I was feeling peckish came just as there was a lull in conversation and my tummy gave me away with a long slow growl. The traitor.

Adriana walked over to me and offered half a stick of gum. She does this constantly. Like half a stick of Juicy Fruit is even enough to get into a good chew without accidentally biting the inside of my cheek in the attempt. I waved it off saying thanks and walked over to the gate.

Wicked followed me and mewed softly as she stuck her nose through the bars.

Suddenly she began to growl, and her fur made its lofty accent as it puffed out, creating a black halo of fuzziness. Wicked's tail began to lash, and her growl grew in crescendo.

"What's wrong with her? What does she see?" Adriana barked at us.

Wicked backed up a few feet then turned and hightailed it over to where my mother was standing. Just as she reached Adelaide, a thin wall of mist separated the rest of my party from me, with the exception of Pandora who was on my side. The sounds of alarm from those left behind seemed dulled by the shimmering veil, and I felt uneasy but not frightened. I think I knew what was coming before I heard the voice begin to speak.

"Well, well, well. What do we have here? A welcoming committee?"

That voice, one which I'd hoped to never have to hear again, sent a cold, angry, shiver down my spine.

"Donna."

"Lily."

"It's been a while."

"It has. I've been waiting for you. I guess you've been too busy what with one thing or the other causing mischief and pandemonium. I was put on your backburner it seems."

She looked haggard and wrung out. Like the months living underground had sucked whatever life she had in her, turning her into a corn-husk doll or a scarecrow of sorts. Gaunt, pockmarked, and sickly, I could still see the crazed look of one who'd lost her marbles eons ago, and the hatred I felt coming from her person did nothing to stop my desire to get the answers I needed from her one way or the other.

"The only one who causes pandemonium around here is me, sugar." Pandora walked up to the gate and I watched in amazement as Donna's eyes grew wide with alarm.

"You!"

"Surprise!" Pandora chortled with glee.

"No! It can't be!"

And with that exclamation, Donna popped out of existence in a puff of smoke.

"Quick. Don't let her get away, grab on to me and let's get her!" Pandora yelled as I glanced back at my mother. Adelaide nodded, knowing what I was about to do, and I was grateful to see she held Wicked safely in her arms. One less creature to have to worry about. I knew my mother would keep her from harm. Adelaide gave me the silent encouragement I needed to complete what I had planned all along. I just didn't expect Pandora to be attached to me. It was too late when Adriana realized what was going down, but even as I could see her frustration at being left out of the battle, I saw the satisfaction and pride in her eyes as I took charge of the situation the only way I knew how.

Well, here goes nothing.

I reached into my pocket and pulled out the potion I made with the essence of Donna's magic. Casting the spell in reverse, I felt myself hurl into some kind of super web of magic, only to pop out on the other side of the gate, landing with a thud on top of my nemesis. Pandora was with me, and her weight pushed me down so I was nose-to-nose with Donna.

"Tag. You're it." I cried. Then all hell broke loose.

CHAPTER 13

I don't think I truly comprehended how taking on a deranged witch alone—with the exception of a crossroads demon as a surprise ally—would turn out, but the battle that ensued would remain with me for the rest of my days. Especially when I paused enough to consider that a year ago I was watching my mother, or my aunt who I thought was my mother, succumbing to cancer and facing being homeless. Fast-forward to a year later and not only was I battling a witch, with magic, but I was shooting spells from my fingertips like a freaking pro.

I didn't have time to react to the fact that Donna, in her maniacal and methodical way, did indeed have a small army. Maybe not to the numbers I feared, but once she grabbed onto me and transported us deeper into her lair, the reality of what she'd built hit me like a two-by-four to the head. Unless Pandora was a super ninja demon of some repute in the defense department, we might be in a tad bit of trouble.

"Where did she go? Do you see where she went?" I was screaming at Pandora as she systematically smashed her way through what could only be called midget zombies. No. Really. It seems Donna could only do so much with the magic she had at her disposal, so we were fighting our way through a quagmire of mindless, tiny humanoid forms devoid of any real fighting prowess or packing much of a threat except in their sheer numbers—and sticking ability. They were like senseless projectiles of walking glue. Velcro-like automatons constantly moving forward and attaching themselves to our legs and each other, preventing any kind of escape unless we dispatched them, which I found my tiny, silver daggers the perfect weapon for.

"Ugh. These guys suck!" Pandora complained as she sent rapid fire missiles into their tiny bodies. They exploded on impact and left skin-like floating ash in their wake. "I don't see her anywhere, and I have no idea where she ran off to. Just keep hitting these things so we can find her!"

Round after round of these ridiculous underlings kept driving us backward so I tracked my eyes to where they were coming from and noticed we were at the top of what looked to be a very long ramp that led downward.

"There is another level below this one. Maybe she went down and sent these jokers up?"

"Good enough for me. Let's try to work our way past this sea of glue and find out, shall we?"

It took us another few minutes of constant stabbing and thrusting and exploding little people until we finally had the majority of the zombies dead, maimed, and/or wandering in circles. I didn't need to look into a mirror to know I was covered in ash and sweating like a marathon runner.

"Nice work. You handle those daggers like a weapons master." I didn't want to preen under Pandora's compliment, but it did feel good to finally be able to toss spells and throw weapons without burning down a village.

"Thanks. You don't suck yourself."

"Naturally!"

We ran down the embankment to the lower level and into a vast chamber whose floor seemed to be made of dirt. All along the walls, arches led to what looked like more iron gates. Wood sconces wrapped in some kind of oil-soaked linen burned, casting a soft glow as they lined the stone walls. It reminded me of something you'd see in a role-playing game. I felt slightly disoriented and queasy and hoped a dragon didn't pop out of the center of the room and attack.

"What is this place? It looks familiar but alien at the same time."

Pandora allowed her eyes to wander over every square inch of the room before replying. "What we have here is an old battle area. Just over three hundred years ago, witches still allowed such things to go on in the prison, not unlike the Roman's did with gladiators and such. Spectacle and drama and all that. That's what this is, a leftover relic from the days when witch families and other paranormals paid good money to watch prisoners battle it out with fantastical beasts and other baddies for sport."

"In Georgia? This isn't flipping *Rome*. This is Georgia!"

"Rome. Georgia. The North Pole. Seriously, people like this kind of stuff, and even when it gets outlawed, every thousand years or so it makes a comeback. We are about due for a resurgence in popularity again," Pandora shrugged.

Not on *my* watch. Not if I could help it. It was barbaric! What if it happened to us? Wait. The gates on the far wall began to slowly open and I could just make out something horrible and big on the other side. It was happening to us!

"Good gracious! What the heck is that?!" I may have squawked a little, eyes wide and yes, teeth gnashing.

"Oh, no."

Let me tell you something. When a crossroads demon says 'oh, no,' the first reaction you have is to turn and run as fast as you can back the way you came. The second reaction is to stay in one spot and begin to pee yourself. I don't know if there was a third reaction because I suddenly found myself battle-charging forward toward something that looked like a rhinoceros mated to a Barbie doll. I think they were female. There were two of them and they were vast, armored, had horns coming out of places no horns should be coming out of and were shouting obscenities.

And they had battle axes that sparked magic.

I raised my hands high above my head and slammed what I hoped were the heaviest pain spells at my disposal. I hit the one closest to me dead on and she didn't even flinch. Not good. Pandora was slightly ahead of me and the beast changed direction and flattened the crossroad demon like she was a blade of grass. The forward momentum of her assault had the creature behind me now and I stopped to help Dorie up from the ground where she'd been planted. Seriously, a Pandora-shaped indentation was now left behind as we ran to the center of the room. We went back-to-back and faced each beast. I was hoping for some kind of inspiration to strike because it didn't seem like magic worked on these two.

A tremendous explosion sounded from up the ramp on the level above, and I hoped it was Adriana and the rest of my gang breaking through the barrier.

"What are these things?"

"They are kind of like gorgons. You know? Like in mythology?" Pandora explained.

"The snake-like women who can turn you into stone? Medusa? Those gorgons?" I asked a bit frantically.

"Yeah."

"But... but these things have legs. And clawed feet and hands! *Clawed* hands with only three fingers. They look nothing like Medusa."

"Technically its one thumb and two fingers. And I said they were *like* gorgons. They are Graeae."

"Grey eye?"

"Not spelled that way but yeah, that's what it sounds like, doesn't it?" Pandora snickered.

"I don't care what it sounds like. I care what these things are capable of and if I am about to be spending the rest of my life as a pillar in this room or not!"

"Nah. That's all stories and myth. These gals can't turn you into stone."

Well, that was good, right? I mean, I can't think of a worse outcome than to be a permanent fixture in this room and still be aware. It would definitely put a damper on mine and Lorcan's honeymoon plans. My blood turned cold when Dorie continued her explanation.

"They are gut masters. They feed on the guts of their victims and use their horns to get at the soft tissue in your body. They start from the bottom and work their way up until you are splayed open like a spatchcocked hen."

My little girl bits just squealed and went into hiding. Well, they would if they could. My mouth opened and closed a few times with no sound coming out as the two monsters circled us and chuckled. At least I think they were chuckling. It sounded more like the grinding of gears than anything else.

I flexed my arms, thanking the powers that be that I

chose to wear the outfit Adelaide had made me. At least I had ease of movement and flexibility on my side— although I had very little on in the way of armor. Pandora was similarly dressed although I still think the high-heeled boots were a bit much, but she didn't seem to be sinking into the soft loam under our feet.

"How are we doing this, then?" I side-whispered, hoping she had a better plan than mine. My idea consisted of screaming and possibly playing dead.

"Just wait it out. They are vain creatures. Before it's all said and done, they are going to remove those helmets because they want us to see their faces."

"So? Who cares about that? Looking at what I assume will be two nasty mugs has nothing to do with how to beat them and win this little skirmish!"

"It doesn't? You'll see," Pandora smiled knowingly. Ugh! I hate that.

I felt mist brush against our skin and wondered at the source. I could also hear what sounded like running water nearby and had the overwhelming urge to strip naked and run toward it to remove the muck and mire from my person.

"We will grind you to dust, puny human."

What? They can speak?

"Say that again? Dust? Human? I am, in fact, a witch, thank you very much!"

"Human, witch. All taste the same to us."

The one facing me began to laugh and beat her hands on her chest. The horns poking out around her armor jumped and thrust out with every chortle. They looked extremely sharp, and I barely stopped myself from gulping out loud. No need to let them see my fear, after all.

"You sound like *Millicent the Slobovian Rabbit* that lusted after *Bugs Bunny* in the old *Looney Tunes* cartoons. It's not a very flattering sound, you know."

I could see confusion cross what little of the beast's face showed through the helmet. Pandora doubled over laughing and nodded her head in agreement.

"You're right! Oh my gosh! How did I never make the connection before? I've run across creatures like these two and they all sound the same! Ha!"

"What is this milli-sent slob rabeet you speak of?" demanded the lumbering monster in front of me. She looked concerned and insulted at the same time, and I could barely hold in my laughter. This was certainly a surreal turn of events, and I knew I could use my wise-cracking mouth to keep these two distracted for now.

"We not luny!" uttered the other.

"Oh, definitely Millicent," barked Dorie.

I guess our teasing had the effect Pandora was waiting for, because the two behemoths whipped their helmets off allowing me to see the horror that was their countenance!

"They have one eye. Why do they only have one eye?" And holy moly was it one ugly eye. Big, yellowish-green with a blue iris that was milky like they suffered from cataracts. The feature was almost overshadowed with the only other thing that made up their faces. "What is with that mouth? Oh, my Heavens they even have lips like Millicent!"

Big, bloated lips flapped and wiggled over nasty little sharp teeth as they grimaced and slid their purple tongues across them.

"Stop say milli-sent. We not this milli-sent."

Pandora sent a level gaze my way and asked me a question.

"Lily, do you know the tale of Odysseus and Polyphemus? How that turned out for good old Poly?"

I wracked my brains trying to remember any and all the Greek mythology I came across and had visions of Jason and his Argonauts, Medusa, Zeus and his lightning bolt, Thor and the like, running through my head. Odysseus was there but nothing was ringing any bells. My confusion must had played across my face because Dorie followed it up with another clue.

"You know, the cyclops?"

Cyclops! A stake! A wooden stake in the eye! I didn't have a stake! I didn't have a dagger big enough to make a dent in those eyeballs. I had nothing I could think of to plunge into that orifice. I had... I had... I had a *sword*! When the realization of what Pandora was saying dawned and she knew I was on the same page, she began the countdown.

"On three. One, two..."

In one fluid movement I removed the sword from the scabbard like Adelaide had me practice over and over again, knowing she'd be proud that I managed to do so. She'd be ever prouder when, on my first strike, I managed to plunge the tip of it deep into the eye of one of the monstrosities lumbering before me.

I expected her to scream in pain. What I didn't expect was her tossing her head back and the result being me being flung over her noggin while still holding on tight to the hilt of my sword. I landed hard on the other side of the beast with a firm grip and rolled to my feet. My sword was dripping with a purplish smear that had to be the Graeae's blood. Pandora lashed out with a shiny black leather whip and dropped the second beast to the ground where she landed face up. Where the heck did she get a whip?

"Quick, do the same to her. Hurry!"

Easier said than done. The Graeae's head was massive, and I'd need a boost up to land a direct hit. She was still holding on to her helmet and using it as a club of sorts that she bashed around on the ground. On her last downward motion, I timed it just right and hopped up onto the helmet then plunged my sword deep, wrenching it a little as I did, and watched in amazement as the beast opened her mouth to howl but then froze.

The ground began to quake, and I held on to my sword to try and remain steady but found myself sliding to the ground instead.

Then those darn monstrosities blew like powder kegs and I found myself covered in more glop—this too of the purple and sticky variety.

Pandora stumbled over to where I was sprawled and slid to the ground near me.

"Did you see the other things scurrying around here while we fought?"

"Maybe? I mean I thought I saw and heard other noises, but I was a bit distracted." I sniffed and wiped my face.

"I take it back. There is an army down here, but I don't think all of them play on Donna's team. The Council is blind and dumb it seems. This place is packed with all manner of beasties and looks to be a virtual breeding ground for them. Someday soon the things that go bump in the dark down here will begin to crawl up into the light —and Sweet Briar is going to be in a heap of trouble when they do."

Oh, that was a lovely thought. I knew the Council threatened to blow the prison to Kingdom Come, but I also knew that couldn't be the answer because what if that turned out to be the way the monsters down here won their freedom?

I shook my hand loose of something stringy and slick.

"Do you think we will ever get this gunk out of our hair?" Pandora asked.

"I'm more concerned about getting it out of my teeth."

Pandora chuckled then groaned.

"Oh, I am getting too old for this crap."

"And how old would that be?" I asked, wondering if she'd respond.

"Who is the oldest being you know?" she asked me.

"Well, I don't know them personally, but Mortimer's parents have to be at least two thousand years old. And the vampire that I saved from Lucretia was easily that much."

Dorie just stared at me and I gulped. Whoa. Ok, then.

"Shall we continue on, then?"

I agreed and we continued our hunt for the elusive Donna Fredricks. At this point, the score I had to settle with her had jumped tenfold.

CHAPTER 14

"If I have to do much more walking I am going to start crying. I mean it. I've been good this long. I've put up with beasties and goo. I've put up with combat. But this walking is for the birds." I complained loudly. I didn't even care if Donna could hear me at this point. We had been following a small stream that morphed into a flowing creek for about ten minutes now and I was annoyed. Who the heck knew these subterranean worlds existed under Georgia? New York, I could almost understand. But Georgia?

"Nomads. Birds don't really walk for long periods of time, do they?"

"Birds! Nomads! I don't care. I just want to stop moving. I ache!"

"How about we float?" Pandora asked and pointed to what looked like a small boat anchored to the embankment up ahead.

"Don't you think that's rather convenient? It's probably a trap. I get to the point of exhaustion and sore feet and suddenly a boat shows up?"

"I've been staring at it for about three minutes now, so it didn't just show up. What else are we supposed to do? Trap or otherwise, at least it will get us moving forward down this creek and we don't have to get wet."

"Fine. Let's get this over with. At least I'll be sitting."

We scrambled over the side of the small wooden boat and took our seats in the middle. Pandora picked up the oar and pushed off the shoreline after untying the rope that held it secure, and we began to meander along with the flow.

"Oh, this is heaven." The mist had built up to a mild fog, but it didn't matter to me; I wasn't walking in it. Nothing could bother me right now because I was sitting down.

I'd just uttered my joy at the much-needed break my feet were getting when I noticed an uptake in our forward momentum. The boat began to speed along, still nice and stable, but definitely at a faster pace than we had been going just seconds earlier. My hair caught the breeze and began tickling my face. Pandora wordlessly handed me a scrunchie and motioned I should probably tie it up, so I did. Whip, and now a scrunchie. Hester and Dorie were positively coming across as Girl Scouts in their preparedness compared to me, although I still felt superior with my nice duds. I cast another look at Pandora's boots and shook my head.

"Lily! Pandora! Get out of there!"

"Lily! Get out of that boat!"

Swiveling our heads back and forth, it wasn't until we looked up to see our group leaning over some kind of railing high above us that we could tell where the warnings were coming from.

"What's wrong? How did you get in here?" I called to them.

"No matter, Lily! Hurry! Get out of that boat!" yelled Adelaide.

"Oh, crud. Too late for that, Lily old girl. Hang on!" Pandora stated and grabbed my hand then pointed to something ahead of us in the mist.

I was just able to make out what looked like a looming cavernous opening when I felt myself tilt forward then plunge, and I realized we'd just gone over a waterfall. How far we'd be going was another matter entirely. I scrunched my eyes closed and screamed, waiting for the crash that never came. Instead, I realized I was sitting on the ground and quite dry, although I could still hear the water around me.

Opening one eye, I found myself in a noticeably modern room with an opening that overlooked the waterfall. Several comfy chairs faced the scenery and there looked to be a long bar on the far side with several doors that led to parts unknown beyond.

This was an odd but welcome respite from the cave-like chambers we'd been wandering through so far. I wondered if this were one of those observation rooms the rich and wealthy paranormal used before a battle would ensue in the fighting area we'd just departed. Unless... I stood and walked over to the window looking down. Nope. No secondary arena below us. Just more water and darkness.

Pandora stood and rubbed her behind. Then walked over to one of the doors. Throwing it open, she peered into a long hallway then went to the next and the next until all were opened and all revealed more of the same. Hallways leading to who knows where.

"Ugh. More walking. Great."

Or so I thought, but just as we were about to choose one of the doors and continue our trek, we heard what could only be someone's muffled cry and a pounding that came from the hallway to our far right. Heading there instead, we found a corridor that ended at a small white door. Trying the handle, we found it locked and I was about to comment on our luck when I remembered my magic. Concentrating on a simple unlock spell, I made quick work of our barrier and turned the knob once more. This time the door opened, and I found myself in a room with...

"Grandfather Antonio!"

WHILE I WAS RELIEVED to find my great-grandfather alive, he was hardly well. Bound and gagged and obviously dehydrated, he sported a rather large bump on his head and looked to have aged at least ten years since he fell in that blasted manhole. And that was saying something considering he was well into his hundreds!

"Goodness! Dorie, help me. Untie his feet while I get his hands free." Working quickly, we managed to release the bindings that held the old man to the chair he'd been sitting in quietly waiting for someone to come along and rescue him. His condition told me all I needed to know about how he was treated.

"Here, Lily. This door leads to a bathroom. Let me help him in there and you go see if one of the other hallways has a passage that heads back up to your family. We need to get him medical attention, although I will do what I can with my powers."

"Shouldn't I help him in there?" I queried, wondering how Dorie would fare in the toilet with someone as old school as Antonio.

"Do you think he'd appreciate having to be exposed to

his great-granddaughter instead? At least I'm a stranger to him!" She had a point.

I hurried out of the room and dashed back the way I had come only to skid to a halt when I found the one person we'd been searching for lounging in one of the comfortable chairs near the waterfall.

"You evil bitch. Couldn't you have given that poor man some water and bathroom breaks? You really are a monster."

"Oh, can it, toots. I don't care if that old man lives or dies. Or don't you get it yet? I don't care if any of you people are left standing after I have my way with the lot of you!"

"Donna. We figured it out. We know you are related to us. But your past, and how you were treated are no excuse for the despicable things you've done because you are butthurt. I mean, really! Did you truly believe we'd embrace the two of you with all the nasty things you'd been up to prior to destroying any chance my mom and dad had at happiness?"

"I didn't care one bit about Charlie and Addie...or Jessica for that matter. Oh, I knew all about their little deceit being a major player in what happened to your family. That was all Deanna. All she ever wanted was Charlie Sweet. Always Charlie Sweet. I was so sick of hearing her moon over that man I would have killed her sooner had I had the chance. I wanted Adriana, that sanctimonious shrew! She deemed me a lesser witch and wouldn't have anything to do with me!"

"Donna! You were the one hiding your abilities. What did you expect her to do? Decide you had a nice, demented smile and train you to be a dark witch like her?"

"She should have embraced me! Adriana should have known I was something special."

You're something special alright. You should ride the looney-go-round you're so special. I knew I had to bind this crazy witch somehow before she could harm Antonio further. I thought to call out to Dorie, but just then she landed an unexpected bolt of magic that froze me in place. Stupid, dumb, me. I couldn't believe I let myself get distracted in talks about the past and didn't just eliminate the threat she posed.

"Still a worthless dark witch, I see. You will never be the witch I am, Lily Sweet. You are so pathetic, I could just..."

Whomp! Donna slammed into me when I used my magic potion again.

"Ow! Stop that! You imbecile! Do you think that will make me release the hold I have on you? I..."

Whomp! Whomp, whomp, whomp!

Over and over, I slammed her into me, rattling both our brains in the process, but at least I knew when the hits were coming and could brace myself. Donna was being tossed around like a ragdoll and started showing some wear and tear. The second I felt her magic slip, I put everything I had into one of the spells my mother taught me, mentally crossing my fingers that this time I'd nail it on the first go. It was time to try the truth serum stunner.

I was about to doubt myself and send out a negative thought, but then I thought of all I'd lost and all I still had going on in my family and I refused to let the negative impact my casting.

I will do this. I thought to myself and gathered the magic, letting it coil up and out. This time, instead of performing the spell as plain old Lily, I switched on the dark witch and knew, without a doubt, my eyes had gone black. I felt myself tilt sideways but this time I was waiting for it. Not knowing exactly what I was doing but certain the extra strength I was feeling had something to do with my siren side, I opened my mouth slightly and took in a huge amount of air as I saw Tarni Vanderzee do. Then I let the magic fly out of me and into Donna.

The air crackled and snapped as my spell rang true and Donna hardened into an unmoving figure as her arms slammed to her sides and her legs locked. Her eyes went wide with shock and remained that way as she toppled over onto the floor with a bang.

I felt only a slight heady whirl of fatigue and where I would have blacked out in the past, this time I let all the air out in a slow whoosh then took in another steadying amount of air and smiled.

I did it.

I did it!!!

"Brava! Liliana! You were amazing, my dear. Steady now, let your dark magic settle." Adriana came rushing into the room with everyone following her. All except Hester who looked to be wedged between two small boulders until I realized she was holding the heads of the Graeae.

Ew.

As she crossed the room heading toward me, a sudden movement in one corner made me jump as a bolt of magic came out of nowhere and headed for a clueless Adriana. I didn't even have time to yell a warning or attempt to block the attack, but another streak of magic came from behind me and crashed into the first one and ricocheted back to the unknown assailant. A loud pop sounded, and a figure cloaked in a dark robe hit the floor just beyond where everyone had entered.

Turning to see who had saved Adriana from certain harm, I found the tiny form of my great-grandfather Antonio, hands outstretched with the look of fury on his face.

His mien softened when Adriana paused to look his way and she ran to embrace the man she'd spent decades with.

"Antonio! Darling."

"Buona...ma, non so se è giorno o notte! Is day or is night?" he asked, his days having been jumbled together for so long he didn't have a clue. At this point neither did we.

"By now it surely must be night. Notte, grandfather." I smiled at the little man who had my great-grandmother wrapped tightly in his arms.

While everyone had all but forgotten the figure lying prone near the hallway, I found myself heading in that direction with Pandora.

"Do you recognize her?" Dorie asked me as she turned the figure over.

"Rowan. That's Rowan Nightingale. Holy moly she's a shifter!"

CHAPTER 15

"Coffee anyone?"

We were comfortably settled in an upstairs conference room the Council used for families of visiting dignitaries whose family members found themselves in trouble with our laws. It was rarely used, but I was glad we hadn't been shoved into one of the small, cold, visiting rooms everyone else was forced to use.

When we had shown up en masse back in the reception area of the prison, shocking everyone present with our capture of the elusive Donna Fredricks, the witch Council was immediately called in. We were awaiting their arrival. I knew Judge Owen Haywood, my uncle, and my Aunt Chiara, Adriana's granddaughter, would be among those present.

At first, the Elders demanded we convene at the auditorium in the main Council building. However, Adriana put her foot down and reprimanded any and all those who challenged her call to have us remain in the prison considering we not only had Donna to contend with, but Rowan Nightingale as well. The former was handcuffed with magical binding to keep her from shifting into something, therefore escaping from under our noses. Although appearing quite sullen, I could detect a small smirk under her glum demeanor and knew we'd been fooled more than once by the girl—but never again. Not on my watch.

Samantha Fairburn was on her way with her sister, Rebecca, who I'd yet to meet. She was Rowan's mother. This should be fun. Why Samantha felt the need to tag along was a mystery, but she'd always been protective of her niece. She was in for a nasty surprise.

The first to arrive was Judge Cornelius Dietrich, and right on his heels, my Uncle Owen. The two contemporaries nodded to each other, then parted. Judge Cornelius over to the podium where he would preside, and my uncle, also a judge, but not in an official capacity today other than being an Elder.

Shortly after they arrived, the rest of the Elders began streaming in. Most looked at us curiously, even appearing friendly. But I did detect a few scowls and outright disdain from a certain sector and knew these were the members in the pocket of the Wilhelmina Dietrich and her clan.

As if on cue, in she came with her husband Boris Langsford, followed by their daughter, Stella Langsford-Plank and her husband Arthur. Stella and Arthur were Edith, my friendly ghost's, parents. Where was Edith anyway? It wasn't like her to disappear for such a long stretch, and I was worried. She warned us of Antonio's accident, then took off to places unknown. I'd have to worry about that later; right now, I needed to concentrate on the matter at hand.

I wasn't remotely surprised to see my cousin, Nora, slip in behind Stella and Arthur. That poor fool truly believed she had an in with the Dietrich clan and chose to align with them instead of her own family. Uncle Owen barely gave Nora a glance, instead coming over to me to hear about our ordeal.

"Listen, Lily. Word is getting out there faster than a Snickers bar at a Weight Watchers meeting. The gossip in this town is second to none. Some people are saying you fought off two giant krakens in an underwater campaign. Another rumor said you performed dark magic and called up a host of minions to smite your enemies. I just want to know if you broke any rules getting to Donna and finding Rowan as a secondary antagonist."

"I don't believe I did anything wrong. I learned of the entrance to the prison second hand via the ghost of the man murdered. What he told Hester and Chester Soule makes sense now that we know Rowan is an evil little snot booger."

"Yes, but will the Elders see it that way?"

I frowned at his words. I didn't give a fig how the Elders saw anything.

I heard a commotion at the entrance to the room and looked over to see Lorcan being held back by some Dudley Do-Good assistant to the Council members.

"I don't care if I don't have an access card, that's my fiancé. So move it." Lorcan brushed past the protesting aide and made a beeline for me. Before I knew what happened I was enveloped in a huge bear hug and Lorcan whispered in my ear. "You have no idea how happy I am to see you in one piece. I've heard nothing but the most horrific rumors since you've been gone."

While I enjoyed the embrace—and let's face it, after the day I had, I needed a great big hug—I could feel Lorcan tense after a moment and realized I must stink like fish or some other nasty.

"You know you can back away, and I won't feel insulted, right?"

"Good. Because wow. I mean, I assumed the worst, but you are going to have to toss those clothes out—or burn them." I punched Lorcan's arm in a playful way and went to take a seat next to Pandora and Adriana who had a tethered and gagged Donna propped between them. She was still stiff as a board. Lorcan went over to the gallery and took a seat, which put him to the right of Nora. He didn't give her a glance, but when Deputy Tiffany—and how stupid does that sound—walked in, he smiled and gave her a little wave. Grr. He really needed to work on how friendly and trusting he was.

Tiffany Clarkston was the least of my worries, however, because no sooner did she wander over to where Lorcan was sitting, than Cousin Nora popped up and made room so they could sit together. What was that about? I thought, after what Tiffany told us, she and Nora would be mortal enemies. How come I thought this little situation didn't bode well for me? Especially as I watched them put their heads together and glance my way then giggle like they had something on me.

Ugh. I *really* hate mean girls!

"We need to call this meeting to order. Will the clerks please set up the recording devices so this is done properly? The last thing we need is to make a mistake at this point," Judge Cornelius requested, and a few workers scrambled around the room setting up little boxes that looked like they belonged in another era, or on another planet.

Olivia Ogden-Meyers, Brian Chase's great aunt and an Elder, approached the front of the room. Brian was at her side and was juggling an armful of paperwork. He did say he was mired in paperwork, and I felt sorry for him. He was being run rather thin these days between working his main job with the state police and helping Sheriff Buford when needed.

Gloria Stillwell and Stella Langsford took their place at the head of the table and the final Elder to join them was Tanaquil Alessi. The room fell silent as everyone waited to see who would speak first.

That honor went to Tanaquil.

"While I understand the concern of the Council of Elders on this matter, I want to go on record as seeing no need for such a meeting to be called. I believe the Dolce and Croy clan have done us a service by not only restoring order to the prison system by recapturing the renegade witch, Donna Fredricks, but returning our beloved past president, Antonio Dolce, from a most horrific kidnapping situation. What more do we need to know?"

"We need to know why the Dolces seem to think it is perfectly fine to break laws and go behind the Council's back in these matters. The Council specifically forbade them entry to the prison lest they create a situation we deemed far more dangerous to our village and the people we protect and govern over their desires," Stella Langsford replied.

She sounded like someone who rehearsed this answer in front of a mirror for weeks. I rolled my eyes and caught Adriana doing the same, and when she noticed mine, we shared a giggle.

"Do you think this matter funny, young lady?" Wilhelmina Dietrich barked a question in my direction.

I refused to answer and gave Wilhelmina a bored look.

"Such insolence!"

A murmur followed that announcement.

Gloria Stillwell cleared her throat and stood. "I think what we really need to accomplish tonight is the questioning of Donna Fredricks. The answers she provides us may give us a lead as to who may have been aiding and abetting not only her, but others who have brought a cloud of evil over our town."

"There is only one family causing all this drama. There is only one family who constantly causes distress and darkness to befall this town. We know who they are. Why they continue to walk around unchallenged and unencumbered by not having to answer for their misdeeds is beyond me!" Wilhelmina shouted. "Now, while they brought this renegade witch back to be incarcerated once more, I don't believe we need them here any longer since this is Council business. A handful of Elders can question this woman. The Dolces can leave."

"I'm not a Dolce. Well, not exactly. I'm a Sweet. And I am not going anywhere," I stated.

"You audacious witch. What right do you have to waltz in here like you even matter to this Council? I..."

"Go sit down Willie. No one wants to hear you carrying on."

Wilhelmina's eyes bugged out when she registered what I'd said to her and her mouth dropped open.

"How dare you speak to my mother in that manner!" Stella cried.

"You can stuff it as well, Stella. I have had about enough of the lot of you dragging your feet and sitting around in your chambers voting on issues unrelated to what is really going on in this town. My family has been under attack for years. I lost my life here, my childhood, my people. I was displaced because of this woman's lies and deceit. I think, more so than anyone else in this room, in this community, I have the right to interrogate Donna Fredricks and get information out of her—and Rowan. I need to help find my father and bring him home."

That old expression, you could hear a pin drop? Yeah. That.

Of course, the looks some of the Council members lobbed at me were anything but friendly now. And Samantha Fairburn was shooting daggers at me for mentioning her demented niece. Tough patootie, lady! Get over it. Your niece is a menace.

"First, I am reeking of filth and muck and mire from cavorting in an old fighting chamber you people outlawed decades ago but still exists in the prison system you keep locked up tight and secure. Why is that? Do you know what manner of nasty is running around down there? Well, I do. I fought some of them off and I won a few battles. I'm sure there are more lying in wait for another such as Donna to come along and promise them some stupid desire they have will be fulfilled, which would have them make their way up a few levels to your cushy offices. Then what? I guarantee there are monsters galore down there you don't even know exist because you never go below and are satisfied with the security on these upper levels. Well, guess what? We managed to bust through your wards and if we can, I guarantee *they* can as well."

I was met with many shocked expressions, but I could also feel a shift in the atmosphere as my words registered.

"Now, while I think it's nice you wanted to join in on my interrogation of *my* prisoner, I need you to get out of my way so I can get the answers my family needs. And I can guarantee one more thing, ladies and gentlemen. Some of you might think you are bearing witness, on the edge of the cusp of change. You think you are looking at the termination of the Dolce dynasty, awaiting your chance to become the leading force in this town. But I promise you, I *am* the future of this town and you better not get on my bad side, because I have a very long memory. And I have decided I like being a dark witch of some substance."

A lone clap sounded in the room and everyone turned to look at who it might be. I scrunched up my face in a moment of confusion when I realized it was Boris Langsford, Wilhelmina's husband.

"If I may?" Boris stood up and gave me a little bow.

"It has come to my knowledge, young lady, despite your predictions and promise of leadership, that you are not who you claim to be." Boris looked around as more murmuring accompanied his words.

"Cut the crap Boris, and say what you mean." Adriana demanded looking wary.

"Why, Adriana, I would be happy to. You see, Council members, Elders, everyone! Lily Sweet is not the child of Charlie Sweet and Jessica Croy Sweet. There has been trickery and deceit galore from this family, and this is the worst of them all. The dark witch, Charles Sweet, did not marry Jessica Croy all those years ago nor produced this woman standing before you. He married the dark witch Adelaide Croy and deceived his own family to hide the mating of two dark witches to protect his offspring. Lily Sweet is twice marked with darkness and therefore a threat to us all."

The room erupted as expected and I felt like screaming in frustration as I watched the look of triumph reached the eyes of my nemesis. I swear, if Donna could have saluted me at that moment, she would have. What's more, she knew I knew it.

My eyes found Pandora in the bedlam that ensued, and she gave me a nod of understanding. Even as I accepted what I needed to do at the moment, I kind of regretted not being able to stand up for myself and my family. But this wasn't the time or place. Not when the urgency lay in the questioning of the one person who held so many of the answers I sought.

Lorcan moved to block me from the throng of people shouting in my face. I leaned forward and whispered my intent in his ear and was grateful that he didn't argue or try to get in my way. I knew I was very lucky that Lorcan was the kind of man who would never forbid me from being who I was meant to be, even with all the worry I put him through. I lightly kissed his neck to let him know how much I appreciated his strength and support.

Then I positioned myself behind him and to his right. Which put me across from Donna diagonally.

"We need to arrest Lily Sweet. She is an abomination!"

"Cut the crap people! It isn't against the law to have two dark witches for parents."

"The shift of power is too much for that family. It isn't fair. And it could be dangerous for the rest of us!"

"How do we know she isn't truly evil and just playing dumb?"

"This changes everything. We need to take a vote on how to proceed with such damning information."

"Doesn't this make our town stronger, having Lily on our side?"

"They've been planning this all along. They wanted power and bred this girl to keep their hold on the town."

More and more words were being bandied about and I knew time was slipping away. Not to mention my opportunity to question Donna before she found herself in solitary, locked away from the world—and my family—once again.

Reaching into my pocket, I took out the tiny vial I'd concocted and popped the cork stopper with my thumb. I gave Dorie a level stare and cast the spell with Donna's essence one more time. However, this time when she was whisked to my side, Pandora was prepared to step in. Grabbing hold of the two of us and facing a shocked room that had frozen when my magic exploded around them,

Dorie did what Dorie did best and transported us out of the prison and off to a place I doubted anyone would look for us.

We landed with a soft thud on the banks of Nichols Pond.

Boy, was I glad the weather had finally shifted toward spring. Because it was going to be a long night.

CHAPTER 16

"Why here?" I asked a rather exhausted looking Dorie.

"Why not? You need to question this one and not have any distractions. This is as good a place as any remote location, or would you rather have me whoosh you back to that hothouse mess?"

Thanks, but no thanks. Pandora was right. I needed to question Donna without interference or meddling. Let them fight over what to do about me, and my family, Donna, and Rowan, without my presence. I was mildly concerned about the revelation of my parentage, but I felt Adriana and Antonio had enough influence to keep me out of trouble. At least I hoped.

I watched as Dorie produced a tether of some unknown material and tied Donna's hands behind her back and forced her into a sitting position on a nearby rock. That's when it dawned on me that my immobility spell was wearing off.

"Don't even try to escape, Donna. Pandora isn't someone to be trifled with," I stated as I watch Donna's eyes move in several directions as if a magical doorway was about to open up allowing a clean getaway. Then my words registered, and she turned to face Dorie then blanched.

"You stay away from me! You demon spawn!"

"Let me guess. You sold your soul and now are concerned Pandora is here to collect it?"

Donna's eyes were wild and intense in the insanity that resided there. Spittle was in the corners of her mouth and she bared her teeth in a snarl.

"I don't have to talk to you, dark witch."

"Oh, so now you admit I'm a dark witch. I don't know, Donna. You were hurling some insults my way a while back, maybe I should just sit back and watch Dorie rough you up for a few. It might make you more humble and less obstinate."

Donna settled down and shriveled inside herself. She looked every bit the lunatic in an asylum and I wondered how she had managed to blend into society for so long. Madness was front and center whenever she looked at you directly.

"Is the truth serum still in effect or do I need to juice her up some more?" I asked Dorie.

"Nah, she is still under the spell. The immobility always wears off first, but you should have a few more hours of honesty out of her." Pandora snickered as she gave Donna a poke in the ribs.

Donna shrank back and snarled like a trapped animal.

"Is Rowan Nightingale under some kind of influence or is she the sociopath I think she is?"

"Rowan wants to form a coven of like-minded individuals and go the path of darkness. She was tired of getting constantly picked on by other kids and she wants revenge.

She was an easy target, but she is not under any influence. At least not the kind you mean."

"Ok. Sociopath it is."

"Where is my father?"

"Ha! Only Deanna knows that one, and I killed her and stuffed her under your porch."

"Pandora! You told me Donna couldn't lie to me, but she just did! Don't try and fool me woman, I know for a fact the girl stuffed under my side porch was a runaway from further south. Where did you put Deanna's remains?"

Donna looked confused then opened her mouth to answer me. "I killed Deanna. I bashed her head in then stuffed her under your porch."

Pandora and I exchanged puzzled frowns. Squatting down to where they were eye to eye, Pandora gave Donna the once-over then shrugged and stood.

"She's telling the truth. Or her reality anyway. Ask her another question or rephrase that one."

"Donna. What do you mean when you say you killed Deanna and stuffed her under my porch? Is she buried under there and we haven't discovered her remains yet? We found a skeleton, but it was a runway that the state identified after the fact. We never found Deanna. What did you do to Deanna?"

"I killed Deanna. I bashed her head in then stuffed her under your porch."

By now I realized Donna was speaking as if in a trance and I felt the heebie-jeebies just looking into her vacant eyes. What in the holy heck was going on around here? One thing is certain, Donna is not the mastermind any longer and maybe not ever. She was showing classic signs of mental illness and had deteriorated even worse from the last time we were face-to-face.

"Do I need to use stronger magic on her? I don't

understand what we're dealing with here. It's like she doesn't want to admit the runaway was another victim and Deanna is not those remains. Hang on. Donna, look at me."

Donna rolled her head in my direction and scowled when our eyes made contact.

"Did you kill the runaway under my porch? The young teenager?"

"I didn't kill no teenager."

"You didn't kill a teenager and stuff her remains under my side porch?"

"Why would I do that when I'd already killed Deanna. I bashed her head in..."

"I know, I know. And stuffed her under my porch," I finished.

"That's right." Donna looked pleased then began to hum to herself.

"I'm open to suggestions here." I tuned to Pandora, but she was distracted with the sudden movement on the surface of the pond. I knew what the bubbling and churning portended and watched as my siren cousin, Tarni Vanderzee, came to the surface.

"Lily."

"Hello, Tarni. I hope we haven't disturbed you."

Tarni rose out of the water gracefully and came over to stand by me, giving me a gentle hug.

"Disturb me? No. Intrigue me? Yes. This is the one who caused your exodus from Sweet Briar?"

I nodded yes.

Turning her head back in my direction, Tarni sidled up to me and sniffed my neck. Oh, not this weird stuff again! I took a step back in alarm.

"Steady, Lily. I just sense the release of siren magic

coming off your person. You've performed siren magic, and recently. How do you feel?"

"I feel fine, but I understand it causes me to black out when I can't control both my dark witch magic and my siren powers at the same time."

"It sounds as if you need something from me, Lily Sweet."

"That's what I was told. I don't want to put you out or cause you any stress. But Adelaide suggested I speak to you about this and perhaps have something to help strengthen the siren side of me."

"And weaken me ever so slightly when I hand over another tear, perhaps?"

My mouth rounded and I hurriedly assured Tarni I had no intention of taking anything that would cause her to lose strength. She smiled sadly at me and removed a pendant from around her neck.

"We are more sisters than cousins, my dear. My time is nearing its end. I am leaving here, you see. My sisters are coming for me and I am not ready to be captured by them just yet."

"Your sisters? Captured? I don't understand. What happened?"

"There's no time for any of that, Lily. It's a sad tale and I don't have the energy to repeat it so you would understand. Give me your hand."

I held my hand out and Tarni turned it over, palm up. She kissed her fingertips then placed them in the center of my palm and I instantly felt a tingling sensation. Looking down, I saw a beautiful aquamarine ring sitting sparkling, where moments before there was nothing.

"This is gorgeous, Tarni. Will it help me?"

"Not yet. Not until I give you a farewell gift."

"Will I ever see you again? Where are you going? What of your sisters come looking for you? What do I say?"

Tarni threw her head back and laughed. The sound stopped my questions, and I felt a wave of enchantment flow over me and make all my troubles seem to fade while the sensation of happiness and calm descended. This was one powerful siren. If her laugh could affect me so, what would her singing voice do?

"So many questions. Don't be troubled by things that no longer matter. We will never meet again, Lily. And for that I am saddened. I would have like to have known you better."

"But why? Where are you going?"

"I am going to meet my destiny. My fate awaits me, and I shall not return. Here. Take my parting gift to you and remember this: you are one of the strongest dark witches to ever walk this earth. Don't let anyone take that power away from you. Not hate, not love, not allegiance, or loyalty to a cause, not fear. Nothing. Nothing should make you give up the power coursing through your body. Embrace it, witch and siren. Embrace it, and be the powerful force you were born to be. Take this ring. Wear it always. Answer your inner siren's call and allow it to strengthen. Don't let that voice be silenced. Ever. Farewell, sweet Lily."

And with that, Tarni allowed one tear to slide down her face, a drop perfectly in the center of the aquamarine stone where it sizzled and was absorbed. Then she blew me a kiss and jumped into the cold waters of Nichols Pond and the surface became instantly still. Then a thin layer of ice crusted over its surface, freezing it solid.

I felt the wetness of my own tears and wiped them away with my hand. Pandora had moved away slightly to give us some privacy, but now she'd returned and placed a hand on my shoulder.

"You okay, kid?"

"I think so. I'm not sure what that was all about, but I feel an overwhelming sense of loss and I hope Tarni will be okay, wherever her path is leading her."

Dorie gave me an enigmatic smile then frowned down at Donna who didn't seem aware of anything that just happened around her.

"What do you think?"

"I think old Donna here has been hit with one heck of a befuddle spell and has been under its influence for decades."

"I think you're right about that."

I scratched the side of my nose then blew out a breath of frustration and impatience.

"So, what so we do about it?" I asked my demonic friend.

"We use that ring you just got on her. That's what we do. I think you should be able to figure out how it works."

I slipped the ring Tarni bequeathed me onto my right hand and felt a surge of power the likes of which I'd never experienced before. Doors in my mind opened and magic flowed through, hitting connections in my brain and merging with my dark witch powers. I didn't need a mirror to know my eyes went black, and I was certain they would remain that way as long as I wore the ring.

Somehow I knew Pandora would say that. Only now I knew exactly what it meant to be a hybrid dark witch siren, and I liked it.

CHAPTER 17

Donna was once again locked, securely this time, in her new home at the prison. Clerics were pouring in from various counties trying to piece together the missing areas of her brain to find out what had happened that caused a befuddle spell to remain in place for so long.

My house was quiet, although the occasional gust rattled my windows. I took a shower with candles on the bathroom vanity in case we lost power. The weather outside had turned once again, but this time it was raining, heavily, and not the icy mix we'd had the past weekend. We were under a tornado warning which had me anxious, but no one else seemed to be getting worked up about it. Therefore, I'd resigned myself to the fact that this must be yet another quirk southerners had. Perhaps a tornado warning was a euphemism for a rumbling thunderstorm and nothing else. I had my doubts, however.

I was snuggled with Lorcan who didn't seem to mind the coal black eyes nor the badass attitude that came with my recently acquired siren powers. I vaguely wondered what the Council would say if they found out about *that* little secret—and forget about the vampire and demon addition. Until I had more information and questioned Pandora in depth, I wasn't telling anyone about my surprise. But in actuality, I didn't care what the Council thought. I'd already informed the Elders I wouldn't bow to any decrees or acquiesce to any demands they asked of me. I strode into the chamber where they were deciding my fate and picked up the mantle my father left for me and me alone.

It only took me three days and one persuasive speech where I may or may not have used my siren voice to have the majority of the Elders vote in my favor.

I was now the head of the Witch Council and president of the Dolce Family Dynasty Foundation & Trust.

Yeah. I liked my newfound power. Sue me.

No. I wasn't going all 'one ring to rule them all' on everyone in town. I loved Sweet Briar. I loved the town, its people, and my family. I would jeopardize them by becoming some great and powerful ruler. Besides, Dorie told me she would stick around and make sure I didn't get too big for my britches. Apparently sirens couldn't influence demons. Pity, that.

"Do you ever think we will find out what Donna did with Deanna's remains?" Lorcan asked me.

"I don't know. I questioned Donna with the power of my new ring, and she just kept repeating herself. I think her mind has been wiped of certain things. No, I *know* it has. But now, I'm afraid to have Abner start digging up my garden in and around that old greenhouse."

"Too late. He's out there right now working on getting your planting done."

Great.

"How does he like the new heat unit?"

"You can see for yourself on Sunday. He asked us over for dinner, and I didn't have the heart to refuse."

"Lorcan Reid! Why did you go and accept that invite? I can't imagine what Abner will serve us, and it better not be squirrel or something like that. All mine have mysteriously disappeared."

"I think that has more to do with Wicked than Abner, Lily," Lorcan chuckled.

"Hey, you two." Adelaide came into the room and paused long enough to greet us and ask a question before heading upstairs to her room. "What is going on with Rowan, Lily? Any news?"

I shook my head no and waited for my mother to leave before turning around in Lorcan's lap so I could face him.

"Did you lie to your mother just now, Lily?" Lorcan asked incredulously.

"Maybe. Yes. Ugh, Lorcan. I don't want to talk to her about any of what is going on at the Council. I am dealing with red tape and bureaucrats in abundance. It's been diffi-cult enough trying to keep Adriana from interfering. Thankfully, she is busy nursing Grandpa Antonio back to health. I think Rita Chase is over at their home right now with some herbal concoction from her shop or maybe it was Samantha who brought it. I don't know, and I don't care. I'm just happy Adriana is too busy with him to pester me!"

"Are you overwhelmed with everything that still needs to be done before this mess is wrapped up?" Lorcan asked.

"Maybe. I'm playing my cards close right now, Lor. Plus, I have a trap set and once it's sprung, things are going to change around this town with me as the catalyst yet again."

"Care to share with me?"

I sighed inwardly knowing that trouble was on the way

and I'd been trying to keep my family at arm's length until I had all the answers. I'd made Tanaquil Alessi my second in command, much to the surprise of my family, who thought I'd choose my Aunt Chiara. But that was just it. I didn't want to be accused of gerrymandering in my new role as president. Tanaquil was trusted as a fair and dedicated witch. Long an Elder, she often brought the calm to an otherwise boiling cauldron of emotions when the full Council was in session.

Tanaquil and I had been working diligently to set a trap of sorts. We knew someone had been helping Donna, and while Rowan seemed the likely candidate, someone had to have groomed the young woman. Samantha, her aunt, and her mother Rebecca, feigned surprise and distress in learning how deeply they were fooled by the girl. Rowan was cooling her heels in the mental ward of the hospital and would soon be sharing air space in the prison with Donna. Never together but definitely incarcerated.

With Donna in la-la land mentally, our hopes had turned to Rowan to find out the answers she may or may not be privy to regarding the past. She wasn't even born when all this happened twenty-two years ago now. But perhaps she'd overheard Donna or Lucretia or whomever is pulling these puppet strings. Tanaquil and I had an appointment with her tomorrow at the hospital. Hopefully, we'd get somewhere with her then.

"Not really. I'm not shutting you out, Lorcan. Or my family. I have to do this differently now that I've taken on so much responsibility. Please understand."

"I do. I just want you to know I am here to help, as a shoulder or in whatever capacity you need, Lily."

I smiled at my fiancé and snuggled close once more.

"What I need right now is to be surrounded by your arms and to have your empath abilities remove the stress from my mind. No one can ease the burdens of this world like you, Lor."

"Your wish is my command, Tink."

Lorcan often called me Tinkerbell as a term of endearment since my other profession is making sculpture art out of found things. That's what I named my shop, after all.

I'd just relaxed into Lorcan's arms and felt myself dozing off when a loud clanging noise startled me out of my reverie. My heart slammed into my chest and Lorcan spilled his coffee on the two of us as he pitched forward in alarm.

"What the?"

"Edith Plank! Are you kidding me? I said a warning. Not the nuclear-testing site fallout alarm noise to announce your arrival!" I'd requested an advance notice from Edith, my resident ghost, before she popped in on me, and her sound of choice left a lot to be desired. It certainly gave us fair warning, but was wreaking havoc on our mental state, not to mention Wicked's.

"Lorcan help Wicked down off the draperies. She shot up there and now her nails were stuck in the fabric. Edith, what is it now? And where have you been?"

"Don't get so uppity with me, Miss President of the Council! I've been working my patootie off for you all this time."

"Doing what?"

"Interrogating Orville and keeping him from haunting you of course! That's my job! You are the one who freaks out every time there is a freshy in town!"

"A freshy?"

"A new ghost, silly! A freshy! I am your official ghost liaison. This way you never have to worry that you will be stuck with an offending specter or have them hang around and creep you out or get in your way!"

Oh, well. That was good, I guess.

"What news do you have for me?"

Edith got down to business and flipped open a little notebook she had in her back pocket. Pulling the pen out that she'd tucked behind one ear, she began flipping the pages and looking at her notes. How she managed to write and hold both the pen and pad was beyond me. Maybe they were ghostly books and supplies.

"Well, before I sent him off on his next spiritual journey, I grilled him but good. Oh! Did you know he was an atheist? You should have seen his face when the escalator appeared to whisk him off to his just reward. I tried to explain that he wasn't going to be judged and wind up in either heaven or hell, that it was an ongoing journey of the soul, but when Saint Peter showed up with a list of grievances, that poor ghost blanched even whiter than he already was and tried to run into Hermione and Hortense's tea shop! I had to scold Peter and tell him to wait his turn before I could coax poor Orville out from under the cash register!"

My head began to ache and I could feel Lorcan vibrate with merriment as he held in his laughter.

"Edith! Stop! Please get to the pertinent information I need."

Edith's smile turned upside down, and her frown made her face go all prune-like.

"Fine. You are such a spoilsport. Orville told me he thinks he knows who killed him. He was about to open the prison and heard a whining sound coming from the north. Since Mortimer and Antonio were to his southeast, they may not have caught it. Anyway, he glanced up and saw a slight form casting the spell that did him in. You won't believe who it is, either!"

"Rowan Nightingale. We nabbed her, Edith. You're too late."

"No, Miss Smarty-Pants. It was *not* Rowan Nightingale. Let me finish! Orville was new to the town, remember? He moved here from Florida, so how would he know who Rowan is? No, he saw a slight figure and recognized the woman who picked him up from the airport when he arrived. He recognized..."

"Samantha Fairburn! Rowan's aunt!"

Edith nodded in approval.

"Oh my gosh! Oh, this is bad!" I shot upright and ran my hands up and down my arms as if to ward off a chill. Lorcan jumped up behind me and ran upstairs to inform Adelaide.

"Come again? I thought you'd be thrilled to know who the real baddie has been all this time!"

"Edith, I am thrilled. But right now, Samantha might be at my great-grandparents house with a brew she'd prepared in the guise of a tisane for Antonio's recuperation. Instead, she might very well be poisoning them! Hurry, we need to go save my family!"

CHAPTER 18

"Hurry, Lorcan! Hurry!" I harassed my boyfriend as I gripped the headrest in front of me. My face was in between the front seats of Lorcan's mother, Eileen's, Buick Park Avenue. We hadn't taken Lorcan's truck or my Jeep because my great-grandparents lived at the end of a cul-de-sac in a huge Victorian. If Samantha happened to be watching the street she'd see us coming. Instead, we took the older black sedan and would park it in a neighbor's drive then cut through the yards to the back of the house to sneak in.

The windshield wipers were making their clackety-clack sound as they went back and forth and back again, driving me mad since I was already halfway there. The rain was torrential, and I didn't see how Lorcan could tell where he was going. I couldn't see a thing.

"Where is Pandora? How is it Adriana could speak with her on the phone, yet that wretched demon fails to give any of us the number to whatever kind of cell phone she conjured out of thin air?"

"Steady, Lily. I put a call in to Mortimer. He didn't

answer but I left a message. Caliente is good about checking it for him. Hopefully they can reach us in time as backup," Adelaide informed me.

"But what if they don't get it in time? Can the three of us take on Samantha seeing as her powers are unknown?" I worried more for Lorcan who had strong empath abilities but wasn't equipped with powerful attack magic or dark anything. This wasn't to say he wouldn't be an asset—his ability to keep me calm and focused in battle would make us a strong duo—as long as I could keep dangerous spells from hitting him.

"Four. Don't forget Wicked. She is an unexpected boon and often overlooked. She is ready and willing to fight," Adelaide chided me softly.

I'd graciously let my mother have the front seat and I was in back with my cat. She was asleep on the seat and looked like she didn't have a care in the world. I envied her relaxed state. I was biting my bottom lip so hard, I was certain I'd break skin any minute now.

The hour was approaching 9:00 p.m. and the storm raged on, lightning flashing, and thunder responding like an old married couple in the midst of a terrible fight. Occasionally, the wind rocked the sedan with its intensity. It was not a night to be out and about, and I hoped the severity of the weather had Samantha believing she wouldn't have any visitors to contend with. I just hoped we arrived in time to stop whatever she had planned.

Would Adriana suspect anything? I didn't know if she'd had feelers out or connected the dots, although I doubted it very much. She'd been too distracted with the temporary loss of Antonio to focus much on who might have been behind all this.

Finally, we had arrived at the prestigious and old neighborhood where Antonio and Adriana lived for most of their married life. Most of the homes were tucked up behind long winding driveways, but a few of them, my great-grandparents included, faced the street in a welcoming way. The neighbor to their right, however, had a long driveway perfect for our purpose. Lorcan slowed and signaled the turn, trying to appear like a neighbor returning home after a night out, looking to escape this weather. We passed the Victorian and continued up the driveway almost to the neighbor's garage doors, then Lorcan turned off the headlights. He put the vehicle in reverse and slowly allowed the car to roll backward down the driveway until we were alongside my great-grandparents home once more.

We'd taken the time to dress appropriately. Adelaide and I wore our special outfits, dark jackets with hoods kept our hair dry and out of our faces. Lorcan was all in black and had a knit cap on his head. Wicked was already black, but unfortunately would bear the brunt of the weather on her sleek fur.

We quickly opened the doors trying to keep as quiet as possible, although with this weather, I didn't think our slamming them could be heard. Lorcan had turned the interior lights all the way down, so the overhead didn't turn on when we exited the vehicle. We paused, crouched near the front of the Buick, and peered through the trees at the side of the grand Victorian. Everything was dark. That could be a good sign or portend something ominous. Either the weather kept Samantha at bay, or she'd already done whatever she'd planned and had left. I didn't see a car in their driveway in any case.

"Do you think someone gave her a ride over? There's no car in sight." I had trouble keeping quiet, yet speaking loud enough that everyone could hear me.

"Who would drive her? Rowan's mother, Rebecca? She

lives in Young Harris with her new husband. I doubt she'd come out on a night like this and give her sister a ride. I wonder if she is innocent or part of this mess? Rowan hasn't lived with her in three years, so who knows what she is privy to."

Just then a loud thunderclap had us scrambling for the relative safety of the porch. I'd lost sight of Wicked, but I assumed she'd already made it somewhere she could stay safe and dry.

"Key? Anyone know if they keep a spare one or have one?" Lorcan whispered.

"I have one, but what if Adriana has a magical alarm system or something. I can't imagine a dark witch locking her doors at night and not setting some kind of ward. Not when any witch worth their spit could open an ordinary lock," I worried.

We crept along the ornate porch, occasionally glancing in the windows when we dared. Everything was dark and quiet. We reached the back door and I looked in. The kitchen was empty. The nightlight near the sink was the only illuminating source. I could see smoldering embers in the fireplace in the keeping room and knew they had to have been there at some point tonight since it had burned down.

Adelaide edged forward until she was beside me and placed her hand on the knob. She nodded her yes once, letting me know that Adriana had indeed warded the perimeter of the house. Then she made a *shh* motion, finger to her lips. Reaching up, she pulled a tiny bird figurine off the ledge above the back door. The bird had a hinged head, and when Adelaide tipped it back, it exposed a cavity filled with sparkling pink dust. Taking a pinch between two fingers, my mother placed a few grains on the palm of her hand then blew it at the lock. We heard an oh-so-soft click and knew the magical lock had been released.

Replacing the bird where she found it, Adelaide mimicked unlocking the door with the regular key Adriana had given me. It would have been nice had she told me about that secret powder bird thingy. I can only imagine what would have happened to me had I came for a visit and used mine, not suspecting the magical ward would be there. She's funny, my great-granny. A real laugh.

Slowly opening the door and slipping into the kitchen, the only sound to reach our ears was that of the many ticking clocks Adriana and Antonio had around their home. Antonio was a bit obsessed about them, so all manner of cuckoos and grandfathers vied for dominance with the mantle clocks and wall-hanging ones, pendulums swinging back and forth. Of course, the clock on the stove was permanently stuck on twelve since no one had bothered setting it. Their old VCR was still blinking that infernal number for the same reason.

We quick-ninjaed through the lower level looking in rooms and opening doors to closets and bathrooms. We determined no one alive was on the lower level. Daisy, the beagle had given me a turn when I found her in the back office, frozen in a happy doggy position. Grandfather Antonio needed to put that thing somewhere where only he could enjoy it. Those glass eyes gave me the willies! Who stuffs a pet? My family, apparently!

Adelaide motioned up, and Lorcan and I nodded in agreement. That was the only logical place left to search unless Samantha had them tied down in the root cellar. Or worse.

Walking as softly as we could into the main grand foyer, we ascended to the upper floor and started down the vast hallway. That is, until I noticed a body sitting in a recliner on the far end of the hallway. I stopped short and gasped causing Adelaide and Lorcan to run into me then look around my body to see what caused my distress. It looked like Antonio and my spirit plummeted. If he was out in the hall, that meant Samantha had done something to him and Adriana was probably in one of the bedrooms—dead.

I couldn't wrap my head around the fact that we were too late.

Holding back tears, I slowly moved forward toward the tiny figure of my great-grandfather. The upstairs was much quieter than the lower level, the clocks muffled behind closed doors. That's why we all jumped and screamed as one when we heard someone walk up behind us and speak.

"Hey, kids. What are we doing? Playing hide-and-go-seek?"

Eep!

§

"WHAT IS WRONG WITH YOU? Are you mental, old lady?"

"Wrong with *me*? You are the one's creeping around my house looking like teenage victims in one of those slasher movies the kids like. Nothing is wrong with me!"

"You couldn't give us a warning?"

"What and ruin the shock and awe?"

"You are a menace! Why did you stick Grandpa Antonio out in the hallway? I should have you arrested for spousal abuse!"

"I'd like to see you try, Squirt. That's where he always sleeps!"

"Why does he sleep in the hallway on a recliner?"

"He gets acid reflux, and the chair keeps him in a better position than the bed."

"Buona notte!" Antonio had woken up and sat blinking

and smiling since the lights were now blazing in the hallway.

"Buona notte, Grandfather. And you couldn't put the chair in a bedroom like a normal person?"

"Qual è il problema?"

"Nothing is the matter, Antonio. Go back to sleep." Adriana explained.

"Sleep? How can he possibly sleep in a *hallway*?"

"Yet he was."

"He looked D.E.A.D. not asleep."

"He was asleep until you came up here and disturbed it."

"You have eight bedrooms up here! You couldn't give him one, so he isn't sitting in a drafty hallway? At his age?"

"I sleep in room." Antonio said.

"See? He wants to sleep in a room. A *room*! Not a hallway!"

Adriana gave me a level look.

"No, Liliana. I go sleep in room. Ma no tonight."

I stopped berating my great-grandmother and turned to Antonio, a puzzled look on my face.

"You usually sleep in a room? But why not tonight? Is it the storm?"

"No."

I turned to Adriana who looked like a cat that ate the canary.

"Well. OK. But, but we are here because we know who has been doing things behind the scenes and..."

"Samantha Fairburn."

I remained rooted in place, mouth agape, and eyes bugged out. Adelaide must have taken pity on me because she finally inserted herself into the conversation.

"How did you know? When did you find out?"

"Oh, she showed up here with some asinine excuse

telling me how concerned she'd been thinking of Antonio and what he'd gone through. She shoved this herbal brew at me, and I could smell something funny immediately. Plus, she kept asking me odd questions like if I'd spoken to you recently or I had any idea what you were doing at the Council with her niece." Adriana addressed this to me.

"But that was enough to make you suspicious?" I asked incredulously.

"No, dummy. Her sister Rebecca called and warned me that Samantha had been acting oddly and was worried she might be more involved than just a concerned aunt. So, I slammed an entrapment spell into her when she turned away and tied her up. She's down in the root cellar."

That's when we heard the bloodcurdling scream.

Then a crash of thunder shook the house.

Suddenly, the lights went out.

CHAPTER 19

We were congregated around the table in the living room. A fire was our light source since the storm had knocked out power for several blocks. Brian informed us a tree had come down a block from my great-grandparents place. He'd arrived with Jake and Becky—those two got stranded down near the Coleman River which had flooded the nearby roadway leading into town. They were out on a date in Dillard and didn't heed the tornado warnings nor the strong wind and rain predictions.

Samantha Fairburn was tethered and bound magically. Her face remained serene, as was her usual disposition, but her eyes flicked around the room, giving away her true feelings.

Tanaquil arrived and I had asked Wilhelmina if she'd like to attend in an act of good faith—something I implemented the second it was announced I would take the presidency my father left vacant. In this way, no faction was left out to question my motives. Wilhelmina was pleasantly surprised to be included but declined due to the weather. She sent Stella in her absence.

Adriana had called Keisha and she had hitched a ride with her Aunt Susanne, the Keeper of Tomes, which also meant she took notes. Lots and lots of notes. Susanne was sitting quietly waiting for the show to start, her knitting needles clacking. She took notes via her iPhone. How modern of her. I know I shouldn't trivialize the severity of this occasion in this manner, but I needed a level of brevity and humor otherwise I just might have hurled myself at Samantha after all I'd been through. Everything my entire family had experienced due to the scheming witch.

Keisha had made some warm milk and doctored it with cinnamon and sugar and broke some of the home-made bread Adriana had made as a treat for Antonio. He was upstairs, resting once again in his recliner, but this one was in the room he shared with Adriana. He'd been sitting guard at the end of the hallway when he nodded off. That was why he wasn't in his room. Adriana was keeping watch in one of the front bedrooms and saw us arrive. I was still sore at her for pulling our leg and scaring us nearly out of our skin.

Every once in a while, I'd catch her looking at me and then cackle.

The scream earlier was due to Wicked having found Samantha in the basement, and taking her frustrations out on the bound woman by launching herself at her head. I promised my feisty feline a fresh bowl of cream as a special treat. Heck, she could have steak if she wanted. The one bright moment of the evening so far had been watching the trickle of blood run slowly down Samantha's face where Wicked's claws had done the job.

Lorcan sat by my side with Jake and Becky on the other side of him. Adriana was in one armchair by the fire next to Susanne. Brian stood and was there in an official capacity to keep things legal. He'd spoken with Sheriff Glen who was more than happy to remain tucked in bed and not have to be out in the inclement weather. Stella and Tanaquil were seated across from us and we all looked at Samantha who stood beside Brian, now looking rather glum.

"So, let me get this straight. You were friends with Donna and Deanna, knew them growing up, and came here at Donna's request when she moved back," I asked.

Samantha nodded but didn't speak.

"After all the drama went down and Charlie ran off to look for my mom, you helped Donna clean up the loose ends?"

Again, she nodded, but this time I detected a glimmer of malice behind her gaze.

"Did your sister Rebecca not wonder why you moved a few towns over following your friends? Or was that a nonissue in your family?"

"Rebecca had her own life and was a troubled teen back then. I was the stable one. I was the one my parents counted on and I always had to cater to their needs. Both of my parents are crippled you see—or were."

Well, that didn't sound too ominous.

"I finally had a way to escape from the burden of caring for them when Rebecca ran off and married a drunk. Once she was out of the house, I was free to go off and do my own thing."

"And leave your parents without aid?" Tanaquil asked.

"They died." Samantha stated woodenly.

Uh oh. I turned to Brian and he stared at me a moment then turned and walked into the kitchen, pulling out his phone. I had a feeling the sheriff in Young Harris would be looking into the whereabouts of the dearly departed Fairburn family. How tragic this all was. Samantha had always appeared so normal, so calm and in control. I didn't know Rebecca well, however, which led me to my next line of questioning.

"Is Rebecca responsible for any of this? Does she play any part in what you and Donna, and to some extent Deanna, have done? I know she is Rowan's mother, but was she aware of any of this?"

"Rebecca? That idiot? She spent her entire life chasing men and getting pregnant. Only to keep having miscarriage after miscarriage—until Rowan came along. That child should have been mine, so alike are we. No, Rebecca is going to be shocked and saddened and good riddance that I never have to deal with her whining face again."

Tell me how you really feel, Samantha.

"So, you've been pulling the strings behind the scenes, helping Donna. Influencing Rowan. Causing all this torment and destruction. And for what? Why are you doing this Samantha? Can you explain?" Adelaide cried, and the venomous look Samantha sent her way had me rising up in my seat a little in case she made a move toward my mother.

"We hated you. We still hate you, Adelaide. Little Miss Perfect. Red-haired vixen. All the men in town enchanted and bewitched by you. Even as a child, Donna told me she'd heard tales about how the three of you, Jessica, Charlie, and you, would cavort around town causing all manner of mischief. While poor Donna had to pretend she wasn't aware of the relationship you all have by blood. We used to play games where we'd make up stories of how we'd ruin the three of you someday. And it built until we realized we had the perfect plan. Especially when you came home with Lily in tow and made the mistake of telling your secret to Donna. Then we knew we had you."

"You evil witch."

"I don't understand such hatred. I can't comprehend the level of evil that must be running through your veins. All this over jealousy? Really? Your best friend, Donna trusted you. Look what you did to her? Why is that?" I yelled, losing my cool when faced with such a vile tale.

"Best friend? I'm not best friends with Donna. Never have been and I never will be. Deanna was my friend. Deanna and I had the greatest time together. She represented freedom to me. It was Deanna who created the potion that ended my miserable parents' lives."

There is that answer then.

"Child, I may be old and get confused easily, but why all this now then? Are you the one who confounded Donna to have her repeat an obvious lie? Did she kill Deanna? Is that why you spelled her that way?" Susanne spoke up with her query.

"Hadn't you heard? Donna bashed Deanna's head in and stuffed her under Lily's side porch." Samantha was laughing outright now, and I rose up on my feet and went the short distance to stand in front of her. No one stopped me when I slapped her face hard, bringing an end to her laughter.

"You and I both know that skeleton under my porch was not Deanna Fredricks. Stop your games, Samantha. Now."

I jumped when a loud ringtone sounded, and I stepped back when I realized it was coming from Samantha's pocket.

"Just in time," she sneered, baring her teeth at me, and glancing down as the call continued. The persistence of whomever was ringing Samantha was getting on my nerves as I waited for the call to end. It didn't, however. It kept ringing and ringing.

"Darling Lily. That call is for you. As a matter of fact, if you let me get this call, every answer you have ever sought about the past will be revealed."

Brian strode into the room and grabbed Samantha's arm roughly. "There is no chance of that happening so why don't you cut the crap and tell us who is calling?"

The ringing finally stopped.

"It doesn't matter. She is obviously bluffing, and I for one..."

Adriana's cell phone began to ring. Not only her cell, but the screen on her computer which she sometimes used to make video calls was also ringing. The caller ID showed up as private, so no number appeared, yet it was coming in as a video call. I felt a trickle of unease run through my body and tracked my eyes to my great-grandmother.

"I'd answer that if I were you, Adriana. It's someone you've been wanting to hear from for decades." Samantha teased.

My great-grandmother rose slowly and strode over to the computer where she touched a button engaging the video call.

It took a moment for the call to connect, and an image to appear on the large monitor upon which the entire room was transfixed. I saw a woman seated outside with a man standing behind her. Surrounding them were hordes of unkempt people in all manner of undress. Some had on torn shorts, others in house dresses or faded jeans. It looked like a scene in a movie showing an old hippie commune. The only two people who were impeccably dressed were the woman in the chair and the man behind her.

I heard Adelaide's voice catch and cried out in alarm when Adriana nearly toppled over.

"Charles," she whispered then sank into the seat. Lorcan rushed over lest she fall.

I peered at the screen but didn't immediately recognize the man standing quietly as the image of Charles Sweet that adorned my walls and photo albums. This man was gaunt and haggard-looking with sunken eyes and a down-turned mouth. The photos I had of Charlie showed a care-free young man who loved life and his little family. This was a sad caricature of that man.

But Adelaide and Adriana would remember. And their reaction told me all I needed to know.

"Can you hear me? I have your precious Charlie, only he goes by Carlito now. I so prefer the way that sounds to your pathetic "Charlie." I have him enthralled you know, so don't try sending out that half-assed spell like you did a few months back. All that managed to do was make him cry and whimper and it angered me to the point of distraction. He is behaving now, as you can see. A few mental lashes were all he needed to get him back in line." The woman reached over and slapped Charlie on one cheek a few times.

"You can forget your plans to bring him home. He *is* home. If you continue on this quest, Adriana, especially *you*, my dear, I will have to unleash your wretched Romano relations and have them descend upon your beloved little town until there is nothing left of it but memories and dust. They may not look like much, but these Romanos have strong dark magic. Heed my warning. The Charlie Sweet you know is dead. He has no memory of you. He is a shell, a husk of his former self, but he's all mine. So back off. But remember to tend the rose bush, Addy."

Then the call ended, the laughter from the woman echoed around the room as it did.

However, just before the screen went black, I caught a

brief image of someone rather familiar moving slowly up to stand behind my father. She caught my eye and winked, just as her hand went up to run it through my father's long, bedraggled hair.

I jumped up and ran over to my mother who was openly weeping and clawing at her face. I gently pulled her hands away from her eyes and hugged her. Lorcan came up beside us and placed a soothing hand on her shoulder and I knew he was using his magic to settle her nerves and bring her some peace.

"Is that the woman from out west? The mystery women we've heard about?" I asked no one in particular.

Adriana turned to face me, and I stepped back when the full impact of her ungodly rage and unadulterated fury slammed into me.

"That was no mystery woman. That bitch was none other than Deanna Fredricks. And I'm going to hunt her down and kill her."

After Brian left with Samantha in tow, and Jake and Becky left with him, the rest of us adjourned to the dining room where Keisha had set out some coffee, tea and biscotti, despite the fact that it was now well into the wee hours of the morning. No one cared. We all needed the pick-me-up.

"That Samantha Fairburn had us all fooled. I took it upon myself to call Rita Chase, considering she'd be short one worker tomorrow, to give her a heads-up. Despite it being so late—or early, if you look at it that way, she deserved to know so she could figure out how to run both shops. Rowan too! Rita has lost both of her workers." Susanne clucked, then went back to her knitting with the occasional grumble and tsking sounds showing just how upset she was by all of this.

Rita had already heard from her son, Brian, but thanked Susanne and offered support to Adriana and Adelaide when she heard the news about Deanna.

Adelaide excused herself and went to use the restroom. She was there for quite some time until Tanaquil checked on her and informed us she had cried herself into a mess. When she returned to the dining room, we pretended not to notice, but Lorcan did go over and give her one more hug for good measure. After that, she seemed to be able to hold it together when we kept going over things.

Adriana forbade any of us to tell Antonio what had transpired. She feared the shock would kill her spouse and I didn't think she was wrong in that estimation. Charlie Sweet looked like the walking dead.

"What did Deanna mean when she said she had him enthralled? I don't understand. What does that mean?"

"It means she has either become a vampire, which would explain a lot, or has the help of one of the ancient beings and they strengthened the magic she used on Charlie when he first left Sweet Briar and morphed it into something he can no longer escape from. He is, for intents and purposes, Deanna's slave," Adriana explained in a lackluster voice. "I better inform Mortimer and Caliente. Maybe between them they can put feelers out in the vampire community, and someone will have heard something about it. Although Deanna certainly pulled the wool over the eyes of many. It was a masterful deception. Masterful." Adriana lamented.

"What did she mean about tending the bush? Why does she need it to be cared for when she has my dad there with her?" I asked, feeling foolish for bothering an openly hurting Adriana with my pesky questions.

"The bush is dying. Hadn't you noticed, Lily?" Adelaide said in a subdued voice. I keep giving it more and more of my blood, but the poor little thing is in distress. I think Deanna was telling me that, unless I sacrifice my life to the bush, Charlie will die."

I remained utterly still for the count of ten as my mother's words circumvented my brain. Then I exploded.

"No! You will not do such a thing! How could you even suggest that?" I cried.

"I'd do anything for Charlie."

"You can't give up your life for him when doing so does nothing to save him from that woman! You need to fight! We all do!"

This was incredible. There was no way I was giving up on my father. Or my mother. Everyone seemed so defeated and all I wanted to do was fight this witch and what's more, bring the fight to her doorstep.

"We can't give up!" I shouted.

"We no give up."

We all jumped as the diminutive form of Antonio Dolce stepped into the kitchen taking us all by surprise. He was in his dressing gown and cap and looked like a tiny Geppetto preparing to work on his wooden Pinocchio. But the fire in his eyes and the strength in his voice showed me this was no man to trifle with, despite his lofty age.

"We no give up. We get Cirino back, capisci? Now we do this-a my way!"

Somehow I think everything was going to turn out just fine. I don't know why I felt this way, but the fierce look in my great-grandfather's eyes probably had a lot to do with it. If he felt so strongly about it, who was I to argue?

Let's give them hell, grandpa!

CHAPTER 20

It was amazing the difference a few weeks made. Daffodils were blooming, dogwoods as well. Pollen covered everything in a greenish dust, and I mean everything. The birds were singing in the wee hours looking for mates and some were already building nests. The air had definitely warmed up and people were out and about, enjoying every minute of it.

The town of Sweet Briar was coming to life as everyone prepared for the grand opening of the new fairground and antique auction house just off the square. Vendors were preparing for the big day and tourists had already started trickling in, spending their hard-earned money on the whimsical and weird this town was famous for.

Many of the folk artists had returned and were preparing their booths with all manner of amazing artistry. Potters and bead artists, quilters and basket makers, there were so many artisans arriving daily I couldn't keep them straight. Even the witchy crafters were setting up shop, with all of their candles and love potions and mystic woo-

woo stuff. Our first spring festival was days away, and I couldn't wait.

Pandora never showed back up. I knew I'd seen her just behind my father and I trusted she was up to something and would let me know what that was when we met up again. How she figured out where Deanna and the Romano clan's compound was remained a mystery, and one for I looked forward to hearing about. I thought it odd no one else had mentioned seeing her. It caused me to keep the knowledge that she had somehow made it across the country and to my father's side a secret from everyone. Even Lorcan.

In the days that followed the surprise video call, the morale in my family was low. I was right there with them wallowing in self-pity, worry, and a fatalistic outlook that wasn't helping anyone. But on the fourth day of my self-absorbed depressive state, Lorcan found me and changed my attitude with one pep talk. For that, I am forever grateful to my lovable lug.

"You ok?" Lorcan was sitting next to me on a blanket on the town square with Wicked in his arms. She had been clingy and protective of my mother ever since that night, and we brought her with us on an impromptu picnic just to give her a change of scenery. I couldn't blame my cat. I'd been worrying and fussing over my mother ever since that night as well. Especially as she'd been spending most of her time fretting over the little sweet briar rose bush.

My garden came to life with spring blossoms every-where. The yard that looked so bleak and uninviting earlier, was transformed under Abner's expert care. Every-thing looked amazing, that is, except for the fading rose bush. Nothing seemed to be working to bring it back to life. It had bloomed but sporadically, and the sickly petals soon fell, littering the ground in a sad visage of things to come.

"I'm ok. Abner is a miracle worker. Have you seen the garden? I have peas! And next week he said he's adding tomatoes and peppers. I'm going to be able to wander outside in a few weeks and pick my own produce!"

A far cry from the girl who used to stare at the fresh fruit and vegetable aisle and sigh while slipping a can of beans into her purse so she and her mom, or aunt rather, could eat.

"What are you thinking?" Lorcan asked me.

"I'm thinking you can't ever judge a book, or a person, by their cover. Look at Abner."

"What? Now?" Lorcan chuckled.

"No, not now, not literally, silly. I mean, we had dinner at his place and who would have known that weird, lovable old pain in the tush would have such a neat and tidy cottage, beautifully decorated, covered in bird feeders and whimsical art—and be such an amazing cook? That lemon chicken and roasted potatoes he made still keeps me up nights dreaming of the next time I'll get to experience it. And that tiramisu. Seriously? When did he learn how to make that? You'd never guess by looking at him."

"No. You wouldn't."

"And Samantha. Donna looked insane, acted it after a bit. But with Donna you weren't as surprised when you finally were confronted with her insanity. But Samantha? Who could have known the depths of that woman's madness? And over jealousy? I just don't get it, Lorcan. I don't think I will ever understand it."

And I tried. I visited both Samantha and Rowan in the mental ward of the hospital and got nowhere with either of them. Rowan had turned into a frothing-at-the-mouth lunatic. She'd focused on me as the reason she'd been incarcerated and went wild when I slipped into the visiting area and then had to be drugged to be restrained. It left me shaken and angry. I still didn't know if Samantha had taken a fragile soul and created a psychopath by years of suggestion, or if Rowan was born that way. She certainly acted like a sociopath. The doctors were astounded at the level of depravity and destruction her shattered brain was under.

Samantha refused to speak to me any longer. Nothing I could do or say would have her talk. Right now, she was awaiting trial, locked away in solitary. The talk was she'd be put to death for the murder of the runaway teenager and her parents. She tried the insanity route, but no one was giving her an ounce of sympathy, not when she refused to show any remorse. I certainly didn't pity her. I understood why she double-crossed Donna. How she and Deanna discovered Donna's plans to eliminate her sister then planned a spell so intricate that Donna remained befuddled for decades was an amazing feat, but even that wouldn't soften my heart. I wanted to see her end. I planned on bringing popcorn.

As for Donna, I went to visit her in prison and something compelled me to let her in on the deceit Samantha and Deanna enacted on her. At first it didn't seem like I was getting through to her, but after about fifteen minutes, her eyes cleared and she looked at me, really looked into my eyes, and in a small voice asked, "Sissy is still alive? I didn't kill her?"

When I confirmed that Deanna was indeed alive and well, a transformation came over Donna that was so disturbing I had trouble concentrating on anything else the rest of the day.

"Then we are all doomed. We're all doomed," was all Donna would say. Over and over and then she began to keen like something hunted.

Yeah. Freaky.

We were moving ahead with a plan to rescue Charlie. Antonio was leading the charge and had been at the Council, visiting with me, and consulting the Elders daily. He seemed to have grown in strength and ability. I guessed knowing his grandson was alive, albeit enslaved by a madwoman, had been catalyst enough to make him want to fight back. The Elders had been most accommodating, and I think it had much to do with my including the Dietrich and Langsford clans in my strategizing. Time would tell however. Just this morning, I heard whispers that the coup attempt was still a foregone conclusion. Some people never got over their visions of power and world domination.

Too bad I planned on beating them at their own game.

And I'd win.

After all, I had the best weapon in my arsenal. Adriana Dolce. She'd been gathering so much dirt on both families, that when the time came for a throw down, they wouldn't know what hit them. All was fair when you had to go to war for love. Especially when you were certain of victory. Not only was I certain of that victory, but I'd already seen the playbook. Heck, I wrote half of it with Granny.

I stretched my arms over my head, then swatted at a fly which had been pestering me going on two minutes now. Lorcan let go of Wicked, who began to wriggle in his arms, protesting her confinement. Once he released her, she began to stalk it. That poor fly didn't have a chance.

"Lorcan look, it's Shirley. She still looks upset about something. Haven't you noticed?"

Following my gaze, Lorcan gave Shirley the once-over and frowned.

"She looks awful. What's up with her?"

"I don't know. But I mean to find out even if I have to

wrestle Brian to the ground and get answers out of him in a tickle fight."

Lorcan raised an eyebrow, and I began to laugh. He had nothing to worry about in that department. My infatuation with the ultra-sexy and incredibly gorgeous police detective was most definitely a thing of the past. Not that I couldn't tease Lorcan a little with it. Just then, a patrol car rounded the curb and parked. Out came the svelte form of one Tiffany Clarkson, of the Sweet Briar Clarksons. She gave Lorcan a little wave, then turned to me with a smile. I was going to smile back out of habit, but then she giggled and blew Lorcan a little kiss, complete with fingers waving.

"Grr."

"Down girl. She's just being a tease, just flirting. That's her way. You, my dear, have nothing to worry about."

Lorcan looked at me while he was talking and didn't see Tiffany give me the stink eye. Nor did he see her make the motion of slicing her throat then pointing at me and laughing before turning and joining Nora in front of Becky's bookstore. But that was okay by me. I knew what games that one would try playing in the weeks and months ahead. Especially since Lorcan was being such a blockhead. I knew Tiffany would use that to her advantage and try to put a wedge between us in an attempt to weaken our relationship.

I had her number.

I wasn't worried.

Nora was back to her old nasty self. I think having another girl in town, and the fact that they had joined forces, had bolstered her attitude, making her less insecure. A secure Nora was not good for my indigestion. But again, I wasn't too concerned.

I laughed to myself when I spied Brian crossing the street and heading into the sheriff's department. He looked up as if he knew someone was looking at him, saw us, and waved. I waved back, then giggled and blew him a kiss. He looked shocked for a minute then smiled, pretended to catch it, and slapped it on his cheek. Then he continued into the station.

"What?"

"You know what. What was that just now?"

"Oh, you know me. I was just flirting. It's all in good fun."

"Lily."

"What? I'm serious. I can flirt and be a tease just like the best of them."

Lorcan sighed and began rubbing the back of his neck. A sure sign he was upset. He pursed his lips and frowned while looking in the direction of where Tiffany and Nora had disappeared into the bookstore, then he looked at the police station before swinging his eyes back in my direction.

"You just did that because of Tiffany."

I opened my eyes wide, pretending I was shocked then hurt by his accusation. I lowered my bottom lip into a pout and replied.

"No, really. I like playing games."

"Yeah. I can see that."

I watched as Wicked ran in a frenzy, hither and yon around the new shoots of grass that were sprinkled among the purple deadnettle and white clover. Then she pounced and proceeded to sit up looking quite pleased with herself. I knew she caught the fly, not just because she had been hunting it, I could hear it buzzing inside her closed mouth. I knew what she was about to do even before she'd decided on it. Wicked closed her eyes into mere slits and chewed the hapless creature up like it was a tasty treat. Who knows? Maybe they do taste good.

Or not.

"I like playing games as well, you know." Lorcan continued.

I pressed my lips together and let a crafty look cross my face. I was laughing on the inside.

"Oh? Would you like to play a game with me then?" I asked with a sultry whisper. I wasn't certain if I used my siren voice on Lorcan, but I definitely liked the result.

I watched in amusement as Lorcan's eyes dilated and his nostrils flared a bit.

"Would this game have something to do with removing one's clothing, perhaps?" He asked me in a low flirty voice of his own, heavy on the gravel, and promising things best left to the imagination.

"Why, yes. I do believe the game I'm am thinking of involves all of that and more."

"Then I'm game." Lorcan declared.

Before he could make one move, however, I took a page out of the playbook of my favorite crossroads demon and slammed a mild stun spell into Lorcan. Then I toppled him backward onto the grass, wiggled like I'd seen Wicked do so often, and pounced—getting nose-to-nose in his face.

Then I smiled.

"Tag! You're it. Now you just have to catch me, Lorcan Reid!"

❧

Continue on to The Sweet Spell of Success